The two men at the table suddenly stood and whirled around, guns in their hands and blazing.

Bullets crashed into the bar beside John, and glass exploded on the shelves behind. John had already started for his own gun when he saw them make their move. It was in his hand as fast as the guns in the hands of his ~~two~~ would-be assailants, and John's aim was more true. John fired twice, the shots coming so close together that it sounded like one sustained explosion.

The gunman in the red shirt caught a ball right between his eyes. He pitched back spewing blood and brain matter, dead before he hit the floor.

OTHER BOOKS BY JAKE LOGAN

JAKE LOGAN

SIXGUN CEMETERY

BERKLEY BOOKS, NEW YORK

SIXGUN CEMETERY

A Berkley Book/published by arrangement with
the author

PRINTING HISTORY
Berkley edition/March 1987

ISBN: 0-425-09647-5

A BERKLEY BOOK ® TM 757,375
Berkley Books are published by The Berkley Publishing Group,
200 Madison Avenue, New York, N.Y. 10016. The name
"BERKLEY" and the stylized "B" with design are trademarks
belonging to Berkley Publishing Corporation.

PRINTED IN THE UNITED STATES OF AMERICA

SIXGUN CEMETERY

1

It wasn't much of a town. Hot, dry, dusty, out in the middle of nowhere, it baked in the sun like a lizard the day John Slocum rode up to the outskirts and read the sign: SIXGUN.

Beneath it, in scrawled script, he saw the legend:

Town pop. 29 .
Cemetery pop. 33
There's more dead here than alive, stranger.

John Slocum slipped his canteen off the pommel and took a drink. The water was tepid but his tongue was swollen and dry. He'd been saving his water, but now he would be able to refill it with fresh in this town. Better yet, he could get a drink at the saloon.

That sounded mighty promising after his long, thirsty ride.

The town was small and fly-blown, a little spot between Quitaque and Turkey, but off the main trail. Slocum stood in the stirrups and looked around. Nothing but sagebrush and shimmering heat waves as far as the eye could see.

Slocum had ridden gingerly through huge prairie dog towns, heard their shrill cries until his ears rang. Now, beyond the scrap lumber of the town, he saw the deep gorge of Palo Duro Canyon slashing through the earth clear to Amarillo, a raw red wound in the earth. Lupines, brittlebrush, and mesquite shared the rugged walls of the canyon.

A rabbit popped up in front of him, ran for several feet along the trail, then darted under a dusty brittlebrush bush. The thick musk of cattle drifted to his nostrils, carried on a breeze that felt as if it had been blown from a blast furnace.

Cattle.

Now he knew why his old friend Barney "Cap" Locke had sent for him. This was Chisholm territory, exclusive once, until people had found how much free land the cattle baron had grabbed, section after illegal section.

Slocum hooked the canteen back onto the saddle pommel, then urged his horse forward with the barest suggestion of a squeeze from his knees. As he rode down the street, the hoofbeats sounded hollow on the sun-baked surface, and little puffs of dust drifted up to hang suspended behind him as if reluctant to return to the hot, hard ground.

Slocum rode into the clapboard town slowly, sizing it up with hooded green eyes, wary as ever of any town he didn't know, and of some he did. It was a one-street town with a few shacks made of whip-sawed lumber, the unpainted wood turning gray, splitting, the houses leaning like the trees at Corpus Christi bent by the wind.

There was no railroad serving the town, so no signs of the outside world greeted him. It was a self-contained little community, inbred and festering.

Slocum examined the buildings. There was a rooming house, a livery stable with a smithy's shop to one side, and a general store that said "Drugs, Meats, Goods" on its high false front. Next door was a smaller building, a saloon, with painted red letters that spelled out its name: Sixgun Saloon.

Beyond the main street, on a long rise, a series of crosses and markers studded the skyline. Some were painted white, some were unpainted, but from this angle they all loomed black against the brilliant sky.

Slocum rode up to the hitchrail in front of the saloon, dismounted, and patted his white duster a few times, sending up puffs of red dust that settled again on the cloth like a fly swarm. A small boy sucking on a red-and-white peppermint stick peered at him from the general store's dust-glazed front window. A woman's hand came from the shadows of the store to snatch the boy away.

"Who is that man, Mama?" the boy asked. The boy was about ten, tow-headed and blue-eyed.

"I don't know," the woman answered. The boy got his hair and his eyes from her. She might have been pretty at one point in her life, but she was old now, old before her time. The sun and wind and the backbreaking life had made a twenty-eight-year-old woman look forty. She brushed an errant strand of hair away from her face. "You stay away from that window. Whoever he is, it isn't any of our business."

"More'n likely he's a gunman," the boy said.

"Oh, Timothy, he's no such thing," the woman declared.

"Timothy could be right," the clerk suggested knowledgeably. He was adding up the woman's purchases. "They been comin' into Sixgun on a regular basis ever since the trouble started."

"I told you, Ma!" the boy said excitedly, and he ran back to the window.

"Mr. Dunne, it's hard enough tryin' to raise a boy now, without you fillin' his head with foolish ideas," the woman said.

"Can't say it's a foolish idea if it be the truth," Dunne replied. "And the boy's gonna have to learn about life sometime."

"Well, it doesn't have to be today," the woman replied. "Now, I'd like to look at some patterns if you have any new ones."

Dunne smiled. "Yes, ma'am, we truly do," he said. "The latest fashions from St. Louis. Just arrived by stage last week."

Unaware that he had been the subject of conversation, Slocum looked up and down the street. A few buildings away, a door slammed and an isinglass shade came down on the upstairs window of the boarding house. A sign creaked in the wind and flies buzzed loudly around a nearby pile of horse manure.

These sounds were magnified because, despite the conversation in the general store, the street itself was silent. No one moved, and Slocum heard no human voice, yet he knew there were people around. There were horses tied here and there, three of them in front of the saloon. Boot heels banged on the two-board walk in front of the saloon and a shadow fell across Slocum. He looked up.

Across the street in the general store, a pair of young blue eyes were looking through the window again. Timothy had sneaked back to the front. His mother was in the back with Mr. Dunne, busy looking at the dress patterns from St. Louis. That left Timothy free to watch what was happening without interference. He sucked excitedly on his peppermint stick as he saw the two men across the street confront each other. He wished he could hear what they were saying.

"Mister, you ain't thirsty enough to stop in Sixgun," the man said to Slocum, speaking in a low, gravelly voice. This was the first person Slocum had seen, and it could hardly be taken as a welcome to the town.

The man who spoke was blocking Slocum's way into the saloon. In fact, Slocum thought, the son of a bitch was blocking out the sun. He was a tall man, half a foot taller than Slocum, thin and muscular, with a moustache that curved like the horns on a Texas steer. He was wearing a yellow duster, pulled back on one side to expose a long-barreled Colt sheathed in a holster which was tied halfway down the big man's leg. He had an angry, evil countenance, and looking directly at him was like staring into the face of a red-eyed, angry bull.

Slocum didn't flinch. "You the travel guide?" he asked dryly.

"Don't get funny. I'm telling you to ride on."

"Thirst don't count, eh?" Slocum's hand wasn't far from the butt of his new Colt .44. He still carried a pair of .31-caliber Colts, percussions, in his saddlebags, but the plow-handled Colt .44 shot true, and the trigger just needed a touch, a breath of air, a thought, to bring the hammer down on the primer.

"Not a damned bit. Right now, you're in no man's land, and you can climb aboard that flea-bit nag you rode in on and go back where you come from. Ain't nobody gonna miss you."

"No man's land, eh? Why is that?"

"Neutral ground. You take one step anywhere but towards your horse and you buy six feet of cemetery."

Slocum's eyes narrowed. There were at least two other men in the saloon. He heard a glass clink, a low voice. Maybe this man was the only one he would have to face in the next few seconds. Maybe those inside thought the big man was enough.

"Time's runnin' short," the big man said. "What are you gonna do?"

"Well, I'm going to overlook the insult to that Morgan horse I got there," Slocum said, speaking slowly and dangerously. "But I'm looking for Cap Locke and this is where he told me to meet him. So step aside, Beanstalk, or I'll go through you."

"Mister, I don't know who you are, but you just said the magic words. Cap Locke."

Beanstalk made his move, his hand surprisingly quick for its size, and the long-barreled Colt started to snick from its holster like a striking rattlesnake. Maybe, thought Slocum, the barrel was too long, because it gave him a shaved-off second to streak his hand to his own .44. Slocum's draw was smooth, and his practiced thumb eared back the hammer in one fluid motion. The click of the sear engaging made a sound like a miniature thundercrack. Beanstalk heard that, and his eyes clouded over before they went wide with surprise. The blade front sight of his Buntline had not yet cleared leather when that hair-trigger snapped back as Slocum's finger ticked it. The hammer smacked into the primer and an orange flash, followed by a blossom of white smoke, burst from the muzzle. The big man on the boardwalk tried hard to beat the bullet with his draw, but for him, time had stopped dead in its tracks. The .44 slug caught him heart-high and blew a hole going in the size of a quarter. When the bullet came out the back it brought half the big man's shoulder blade with it, and left an exit wound big enough to poke a ball bat into.

Beanstalk's eyes glazed and he staggered backward, crashed through the batwing doors, and backpedaled into a table before coming down on it with a crunch that turned it into firewood. He landed flat on the floor, his gun arm thrown to one side, the still unfired Buntline in his hand. His mouth was open and a little sliver of blood oozed down his chin. Though his body was still jerking a bit, his eyes were open and unseeing.

Timothy gasped at what he saw. In his childish imagination he was playing out just such a scene, but to see it really happen before his own eyes was unbelievable. He looked around quickly and saw his mother and Mr. Dunne coming toward the front, drawn by the sound of the gunshot, but it was too late. She couldn't pull him away now; it had already happened. It had happened, and he had seen it.

Slocum bounded up on the boardwalk, then bulled into the saloon, a wisp of smoke curling from the barrel of his Colt. He was ready in the event anyone inside wanted to back the big man's play.

In the saloon the two hardcases standing by the bar were caught by surprise. They stood there, staring awestruck at the twitching giant lying in the V of the broken table. Slocum thumbed back the hammer once again, and when the men heard the click, they looked up at him.

"Anyone else?" Slocum asked menacingly. The barrel of his pistol was pointing toward them, holding them still with its one deadly eye.

"Shit," one of the hardcases said in disbelief. "That there's Earl Bagget you done kilt."

"You a friend of his?" Slocum wanted to know.

"We was pards."

"Your pard threw down on me," Slocum said.

"Never saw no one beat him before," the man said, still awestruck.

"Earl Bagget, huh? What about you? You got a name?" Slocum emphasized his request with a poke of the pistol in the man's direction.

"Yeah, sure I got a name. Ever'one's got a name."

"Let's hear it."

"Hamrick. Luke Hamrick." Hamrick was the taller, thinner of the two men. He wore a bushy moustache which though black, was laced with some gray. He looked to be about forty.

"You?" Slocum asked the other man, moving the pistol toward him.

The second was a keg-shaped man of about twenty-five, clean-shaven, with long curly hair that just touched his shoulders.

"Name's Bill Newcastle, if it's any of your business," the younger man said, trying to find some courage in the situation.

"Maybe not, Newcastle, but I want one of you jaspers to tell me why this tall drink of alkali water threw down on me."

"Whatever the reason, I reckon he felt like he had the right," Hamrick said.

"The right? What would give him the right to brace a perfect stranger like that? I never saw him before in my life."

"Mister, he was the town marshal," Newcastle said. "You just kilt yourself an officer of the law."

2

"Ma! He shot 'im!" Timothy shouted. "I saw it, Ma! The man that just rode in, he shot the other fella. He shot 'im dead!"

Timothy started for the door but his mother grabbed him and pulled him back.

"What happened, Timothy?" Dunne asked, brushing his thin hair back across the top of his head.

"A big man come out of the saloon and they was talkin'," Timothy explained. "Don't know what they was talkin' about, but the next thing was they was both goin' for their guns."

"Both?" Dunne asked. "At the same time?"

"Why are you asking him such questions?" Timothy's mother demanded. "He's just a boy."

"Mrs. Abernathy, it might come up in an inquest

11

whether or not it was murder or a fair fight," Dunne said. "What the boy seen will be important."

"Inquest?" Mrs. Abernathy scoffed. "In Sixgun? This is a lawless town, Mr. Dunne, and you know it. People kill each other all the time and the law does nothing about it."

"Nevertheless, it's good to know what really happened," Dunne said. "We need to know whether we got us a cold-blooded killer on our hands, or just a man that was pushed into a fight."

"He can't have been pushed very hard," Mrs. Abernathy said. "He just got here."

"Oh, my, I suppose I'd better get a coffin out of the back room." Dunne said, clapping his hands together as if it had just occurred to him. It appeared, though, to be an expression of joy over the prospect of selling a coffin.

Across the street in the saloon, John Slocum was looking down at the body of the man he had just killed. Bagget's eyes were still open, though one of them was drooping now. His arm was stretched out to one side, the long-barreled gun still in the hand, the thumb frozen just over the hammer. His duster had fallen open so John could see his vest and shirt.

"You said this man was the law?"

"That's right, mister."

"I don't see any badge," Slocum said.

"Don't mean nothin' that he ain't got no badge," Hamrick said. "You done walked into a full-fledged range war, and Bagget was supposed to keep out any new guns until the smoke settles."

"Town council appoint him?" Slocum asked.

"Not exactly," Hamrick replied. "Fact is, we don't

exactly have a town council."

"Who, then? The county sheriff? The Texas Rangers?"

"No, it weren't none of them either. It was a feller name of Tucker Scarns, an important man in these parts."

"I see," Slocum said. He slipped his pistol back into his holster. Neither Hamrick nor Newcastle had made any indication that they might go for their guns, and even if they did, he figured he could beat them. A man gave away a lot in the first two minutes of conversation. "You say there's a range war going on?"

"That's right, mister, and you done landed smack in the middle of it."

"Who's fighting this war?" Slocum wanted to know.

"Feller by the name of Tucker Scarns for one."

"Tucker Scarns. The important man who appointed this jasper the law," Slocum said.

"That's right."

"Who else is fighting?"

"The other feller is Cap Locke," Hamrick answered.

"Cap Locke?"

"You say that like you know him."

"I do know him. How big is this war?"

"They's as many as a dozen men gettin' shot out of their saddles at any given moment," Newcastle advised him.

"Who has the advantage?"

"Iffen you was to ask me, I'd have to give the edge to Scarns," Hamrick said. "Most of them that's left is ridin' for him. Us'ns among 'em."

"Yeah, I figured as much," John said.

"You aimin' to join up with Locke, or with us?" Newcastle asked.

Slocum stepped over to the bar, then looked back toward Bagget. He slapped a coin down on the bar.

"Right now, I aim to get the drink this fella told me I couldn't have," he said.

The barkeep, who had been cowering at the far end of the bar, now slid down the length of the bar toward Slocum. He picked the silver up, put a bottle and glass in front of Slocum.

John Slocum poured himself a drink, then turned his back to the bar and looked out over the saloon. He had been concerned only with the two galoots with Bagget, but now he could look around to see who else was in the saloon. He saw a table in the far corner, with cards and coins spread out on the green cloth. The players were back against the wall, having abandoned their game when the shooting started. Now, with the shooting over, they returned to the game and conversation. One of them laughed nervously.

There were some women there too. One was standing by a broken-down piano, another sat on a sofa beneath the fly-blown calendar. Both were heavily painted and hard-looking. They looked like stone sculptures with rouge on their faces, charcoal-black lines thick as ink framing their eyes. At the back of the saloon a stairway led up to a second-floor balcony, and a hallway led off the balcony to an extension at the rear. A third woman stood on the balcony, looking over the railing. She was younger and prettier, than the other two, and she smiled down at John

Slocum in an obvious invitation for him to come up and join her.

So, he thought, this was why Cap had sent for him. Cap was badly outnumbered and he needed John's help. It was a reasonable request. They had both fought with Quantrill and once, when John had his horse shot from under him, Cap had ridden back for him, braving the Yankee fire to lean down and offer his hand so John could leap on behind. Bullets had whistled by, punctured their hats, pierced the sleeve of John's coat, but neither of them had been wounded. If Cap Locke needed John's help, he was more than willing to give it. He just hoped this episode would come out as well.

Cap was one of those who got good sense, quit the outlaw band, tried to go straight after the War, and had. He had built up a herd from Texas strays, brought in some of the English Herefords, and mixed-bred them with the longhorn stock. Then, following Chisholm's lead, he had come to the panhandle, where he could run them on the big spaces.

Cap wrote Slocum a letter a month ago, asking for his help. The letter caught up with John in Laredo, said that his wife, Earline, had died, and that he had a daughter who was about more than he could handle.

John remembered Earline, all eyes and smile, a woman who had made the best apple pie he had ever eaten. She was a good woman, and John always figured she had more to do with Cap leaving the outlaw trail than anyone or anything else.

Now Cap was left with the business of raising a little girl by himself. He'd said she was about more than he could handle. Strangely, he hadn't mentioned the range war.

"How long's this war been going on?" John asked.

Hamrick was on his knees, going through Bagget's pockets, so Newcastle answered.

" 'Bout ten days."

The letter had reached John twenty days ago. That was why there was no mention of the range war. Slocum was glad of that. He didn't think Cap would be the kind of man to get him down here under false pretenses.

"Who was here first? Locke or Scarns?"

"Makes no difference," Newcastle said. "Tucker Scarns's got the muscle and there ain't no legal claim to the land where Locke runs his beef. That means whoever's strongest has the right to it."

"Ah, here it is," Hamrick said. He took a wad of money from Bagget's pocket. "Sumbitch owed me twenty dollars." He started counting the money.

"Leave enough to bury him," Slocum said.

"Shit, let the county do that. He's no concern of mine," Hamrick said.

"You said you were pards."

"No more, we ain't."

"Get him in the ground," Slocum said coldly.

"Why the hell you so concerned about him, mister? He tried to kill you."

"At least he faced me like a man," John said. "I've had them that tried to drygulch me, and when I can I even see to it that they are buried. Now you two get out of here, and take him with you."

"He's too big to carry," Hamrick said. "We'll have to send back for him."

"Take him now."

"How we gonna do that?"

"Figure out a way."

Hamrick looked at Newcastle, then growled. "All right, you get one leg, I'll get the other, 'n' we'll drag the big sumbitch out."

Hamrick and Newcastle started dragging the body across the floor. A wide trail of blood smeared out from the big exit wound in Bagget's back.

"Hey! Look what a mess you're makin' on my floor!" the barkeep complained. "Who's gonna wanna come drink with that mess on the floor?"

"Yeah, well, that's what a .44 will do to you, Tom," Hamrick said. "If I was you, I'd get it cleaned up."

Tom, the barkeep, brought a bucket of water and a rag around front, then got on his hands and knees and started wiping up the floor, swearing under his breath as he did so.

"Damn me if you don't look like a fella that knows what he's doin' down there," Newcastle chuckled.

"Hamrick, Newcastle?" Slocum called.

"Yeah?" Newcastle answered. By this time they had gone as far as the batwing doors, each hanging onto a leg.

"You asked me who I'd be fighting for. I just thought I'd let you know that I'm siding with Locke in this war."

"You're makin' a big mistake, mister," Newcastle said.

"Is that a fact?" John replied easily. "We'll just have to see about that. In the meantime, since you two said you're with Scarns, why, that just naturally puts us on opposite sides."

"I reckon it does," Hamrick agreed.

"I'm giving you fair warning now," Slocum said. "If I ever see either one of you again, you can slap leather."

"We'll keep that in mind, mister," Hamrick said.

John watched them until they disappeared through the door, and he could hear the scraping sound of the body being dragged along the boardwalk which ran in front of all the buildings.

So, there was a range war. John Slocum had seen it happen before. Cap must have the water, and Scarns nothing but dirt. In these wars there was never any permanent winner. The strongest won, and the other was pushed out. The land belonged to the winner, at least until someone else came along and threw down the challenge.

"Can't say that fella didn't need killin'," the barkeep said as he finished wiping up the blood. "But I wish you'd done it out in the street."

"I didn't have it planned," John answered. "That means I didn't get to choose where he threw down on me."

"I reckon you're right."

"They called you Tom?"

"That's right. Tom Maloney."

"Which side you staked out on, Tom Maloney?"

"I ain't got no side," Tom answered. "I'm just the barkeep."

"You said Bagget needed killing?"

Tom poured John another drink.

"This fella, Bagget," Tom started. "He come into town two, maybe three days ago. First time I ever seen him."

"I thought Hamrick said he was the marshal."

"He was if you believe Tucker Scarns," Tom said. "'Course, like Hamrick said, Scarns has all the money and the muscle around here, so if he takes it on hisself to appoint Bagget the town marshal, I reckon that made him the marshal. It was about as close to the law as anyone got around here."

"What were Bagget's duties?" John asked.

"Real simple. He was supposed to keep out any guns Locke hired. He's already killed three of 'em. Their graves are still fresh, out there in the cemetery."

"Locke know that his men have been killed?"

"Hell, mister, I doubt that Cap Locke even knows they showed up yet. He's been too busy trying to keep the wolves at bay."

"I see."

"You asked me whose side I was on. Like I said, I ain't got no side, a fella like me can't afford to have no side. But, truth to tell, iffen I was to have to pick a side, I reckon I'd pick Cap Locke. He's a decent sort of man who didn't give nobody no trouble till this here range war commenced."

"Cap told me he'd meet me here in this saloon," John said.

"Reckon he will," Tom answered. "He always comes into town on Tuesday, and this here's Tuesday."

"Did Bagget know Cap came in every Tuesday?"

"I reckon he did," Tom said. "I reckon Hamrick and Newcastle told him."

"They were waiting for him, then, weren't they?"

"I reckon maybe they were at that," Tom said.

"I don't like those two," Slocum observed.

"You'll see them again," Tom cautioned. "They'll get word back to Scarns that you killed Bagget, run them out of town."

"Maybe that'll bring Scarns in and we can get this over with," John suggested.

"Not likely you'll see Scarns right away. He likes to get others to do his fightin' for him, like Bagget and these two."

"If Bagget was the marshal, who's ramrodding Scarns's outfit?" John asked.

"The ramrod's a man called Preacher Jack."

"Preacher Jack? Medium height, slim, has a scar on his face, always dresses in black?"

"Yeah, that's him," Tom said. "You know him?"

"I know him."

"I wonder," Tom said. "Is that fella really a preacher?"

"He's no man of the cloth and he never has been," John Slocum said. "He's a cold-blooded killer."

"Why they call him Preacher Jack? Because of the way he dresses, always in black?"

"That," John said, "and the fact that he always says some Bible thing before he puts a man's lamp out."

"They say he's a lot faster than Bagget," Tom said. "And Bagget was the fastest I ever seen till you come around. You the measure of this Preacher Jack fella?"

"I don't know," John said.

"Well, I reckon you'll find out soon enough," Tom said.

"What makes you think that?"

"Once word gets back that you killed Bagget, run two of his men out of town, Preacher Jack will be comin' in to settle the score hisself. If you don't think you're fast enough, you better hightail it on outa here."

"I told you, I'm waiting for Cap Locke."

"Yeah? Well, it's your funeral, mister."

3

The doors of the saloon swung open and a tall, slim man wearing wire-rim glasses and a white apron came inside. He ran his hands across the top of his head which, at first glance, looked bald, but upon closer inspection, revealed several thin strands of very light hair.

"My name is Dunne, sir. Marcus Dunne," he said to John Slocum. "I own the general store across the street. I just want you to know that I was a witness to the entire thing and if it ever comes to it, I'll be glad to testify that it was a fair fight. You both commenced your draw at the same time. You was just faster than Bagget."

"Thanks," John said.

"Uh, I want to thank you, too, for seein' to it that he is bein' buried proper."

"You a friend or relative?" John asked, confused as to why he would care whether Bagget was buried or not.

Tom Maloney chuckled. "Better'n that," he said. "Dunne runs an undertakin' parlor behind his store."

"Well, it ain't just that," Dunne insisted. "I'm just glad to see any citizen get a decent burial, that's all."

"I'm glad I could oblige," John said.

"Anything else I can do for you, mister? Anything at all?" Dunne asked.

"No, thanks," John said. The man's fawning obsequiousness was beginning to grate on Slocum's nerves.

"If so," the man went on, "I can be found anytime, just across the street in my store. I have boots, leather goods, good shirts and pants. Anything you might need."

"I'll keep you in mind," John said.

Dunne smiled again, then backed out of the door. John turned back toward the barkeep. "You have any idea where a man can get a bath?" John asked.

"A bath?" the barkeep answered in surprise.

John slapped the white duster he was wearing and a small cloud of red dust drifted up.

"I've been eating trail dust for the better part of three weeks," John said. "I don't aim to meet an old friend looking and smelling like a mountain goat. I want a bath and a shave."

"Well, as far as barberin' goes, he just left."

"Dunne?"

"Dunne."

"No thanks. Anyone else?"

"Ole' Pop Tarley barbers a little now 'n' ag'in. But he ain't no regular barber. He generally just sets a body in a chair over there in the corner."

"That's regular enough for me," John said. "What about the bath?"

"I got a back room here. I reckon I could sell you the fixin's for a bath."

"Good," John said. He slapped another silver coin on the bar. "Tell Pop Tarley to meet me back there."

Ten minutes later, John Slocum was sitting in a large oaken bathtub, happily scrubbing away the residue of the long ride. A change of pants and a clean shirt lay draped across a chair beside him. A cigar was elevated at a jaunty angle from his face, freshly lathered by a gnarled collection of wrinkled skin and rattling bones called Pop Tarley.

The door opened and a young woman walked in. She was the same woman John had seen staring down at him from the balcony.

"My name's Kate," she said. "I work here." Kate leaned against the door, thrusting one hip out provocatively. She had saucy, auburn curls which hung to her shoulders, and bright blue eyes. The green satin dress she wore was cut so low that her breasts were visible almost all the way to the nipples.

John frowned at her. "Does that give you the right to just walk in on a man's bath?"

Kate smiled. "I thought I might have something you need," Kate said in a low, sultry voice.

Pop Tarley began stropping his razor.

"I've got everything I need right here," John said pointing to the old man.

"Pop? He's too old."

"Pop's not old," John said.

"He's Methuselah," Kate countered. "How old are you, Pop?" she asked. "Seventy? Eighty, maybe?"

"Not as old as the hombre this fella just shot," Pop answered.

"What? What do you mean? Bagget wasn't more than thirty-five," Kate said.

"Bagget's dead," Pop answered dryly. Pop pulled the skin of John's cheek to one side and drew the blade down. "You don't get 'ny older than dead. I'm not dead, so I'm younger."

John laughed.

The door opened again, and the barkeep came in.

"Here's your change," Tom said. "'Course, if you want, I can get you some lilac water. You've got just enough change comin' to cover it. The ladies all like the lilac water. You like it, don't you, Kate?"

"I like it on a dance-hall dandy," Kate said. "I don't care for it on a real man."

"Will you two just get the hell out of here and let me have my bath in peace?" John demanded.

"Pardon me, I understand Mr. John Slocum is back here," a new voice said, and a fourth person came into the room.

"What the hell's going on here?" John shouted. "Can't you people see I'm taking a bath?"

"My goodness, we can all see that, honey," a woman's voice trilled mirthfully from the saloon, and her comment was followed by a raucous chorus of laughter. John craned his neck around the people grouped near his tub and realized that he was indeed visible to any of the saloon patrons who cared to look in his direction, since the door was wide open.

"Pop?" he asked.

"Yep?"

"You finished with me?"

"Yep."

"Good. How about you take Kate and the lilac-water pusher, here, and clear out?"

Pop drew his ancient bones up with dignity, then started ushering the other two out.

"And you," John said to the newcomer, "close the damn door."

The newcomer closed the door, then turned around and laughed a full, rich laugh. He was actually a couple of years younger than John, but he looked older. His hair was white, his face weathered.

"Damn, John, if I'd known you was gonna put on a show I would'a tried to get here earlier," he said, whooping and slapping his knees.

Even John could see the humor of it now, and he laughed good-naturedly. "Hello, Cap," he said, sticking his hand out. "It's been a long time."

"I'm glad you could come," Cap answered, shaking Slocum's hand.

"You sure picked yourself an out-of-the-way place to settle," John said.

"It's not all that bad," Cap answered. "Hell, we've got all the conveniences of a big city. Baths," he ran his hand through John's bathwater, "liquor, women, and food. What more could a man ask for?"

"Ah, yes, what more indeed?" John replied sarcastically. "Let me get dressed, and then we can talk."

John stepped out of the tub and began drying himself off. His well-muscled, finely formed body was covered with a network of scars from the knife and bullet wounds he had sustained over the years, some during the War, more since.

Once he was dressed, John and Cap returned to the bar, where the crusty ex-soldier bought them both a drink.

"Quite a little town here," John said, opening the conversation.

"I guess you heard we've got ourselves a war going," Cap said.

"Yeah," John answered. "I seem to have landed right in the middle of it. There was a big, disagreeable fella didn't want me around."

"Oh? What happened?"

"Man by the name of Earl Bagget greeted me at the door," John said. "Soon as he heard your name, he drew on me. I had to kill him."

"Whew," Cap whistled. "I wasn't sure it had gone that far yet. Well, better him than you. I'm curious, though. I was supposed to meet three other men here today also. They know why they're here, and they're going to be working for me. I'm surprised they didn't take a hand in it, help you out some."

"From what I understand, they didn't have a chance. Bagget put them under yesterday."

"All three of them?" Cap asked in a small voice.

"Yeah, all three of them."

Cap was silent for a long moment. He took a drink, then turned to John. "Look, John, I don't want you thinkin' I brought you here without givin' you a word about what was goin' on. You want to turn around and leave now, why you're free to do it and I won't think the less of you for it."

"I'm not goin' anywhere, Cap."

"The truth is, when I wrote you, I didn't know about all this."

"I know. Newcastle and Hamrick told me the war's only been going on about ten days. So it started after I got your letter.

"I'm glad you understand that. Who the hell are Newcastle and Hamrick?"

"Couple of hardcases riding for Scarns."

"Do you know Scarns?" Cap asked.

"No. Do you?"

"Oh, yeah. You can't live in this part of the country and not know Scarns. He's thrown a long loop and bullied small ranchers and farmers out of his way until he's made himself quite a power. Now I'm the only one standing between him and control of the entire range. That's particularly galling to Scarns, because I also happen to control most of the water."

"Figured it would be something about like that," John answered.

"Like I say, if you want to turn around and go back, I can understand," Cap said, making the offer a second time.

John smiled. "When I was lying on the ground back in Missouri and I saw you coming for me, I didn't want you to turn around. I was yelling like hell for you to hurry up."

Cap laughed. "I was young and foolish then," he said. "You don't have that excuse now."

"No matter. I don't intend to abandon you to Scarns or Preacher Jack."

"You know about Preacher Jack too?"

"The barkeep told me about him."

"He's a mean one," Cap said.

"Yeah."

"Ever met him?"

"Yeah."

"Ever see him in action?"

"Once," John said. "Up in Laramie. He shot down three cowhands who got drunk and called him out. He quoted Scripture while he was doing it."

"Yeah, that's him, all right. There ought to be a special place in hell for people who kill in the name of the Lord."

"I suppose there is," John said.

Cap tossed his drink down, then wiped the back of his hand across his mouth. "Well, John, if you are going back out to the ranch with me, I suppose we'd better get busy. We've got a few supplies to pick up."

"Where is your ranch?" John asked, after they were outside the saloon.

"It's about seven miles from here, in the hills above Palo Duro Canyon."

"I've ridden through that country. It's nice up there."

"Oh, it's a beautiful spread, John. Wait till you see it. You'll go giddy with it, just like I did."

John laughed. "I've got to hand it to you, Cap. I never thought you could leave the outlaw trail as easy as you did. I'm proud of you, coming out here and making a place for yourself."

"Easy?" Cap replied. "Don't fool yourself, it wasn't easy. You don't know what it's like out here . . . wintertimes, a blue norther comes down and it gets so cold a cow's milk freezes up in her teats so that she swells up 'n' dies, and then the calves die. The snows come and the cattle can't find food, so lots of 'em starve. And half the ones that don't starve, wind up freezin' to death.

"Then comes springtime and the snow thaws and the rains come and we're in the midst of high water.

My barn's floated away three times, my house once. Those cattle that can't find high ground get caught in a flash flood in the gullies and you lose half the herd that survived the winter, by drownin'.

"After that comes the summertime. Two months into summer you'd give everything you own for one good rain, and you remember all the water from spring and you cuss a blue streak but it don't help none, and it don't help the cattle. You lose a lot more to the drought.

"Throw in a few diseases, some wolves, mountain lions, and rustlers, and that takes out another good bunch, and it leaves you with a pretty good picture of what ranchin' is all about. And now, on top of all that, there's this Tucker Scarns comin' along to make more trouble. You still want to tell me how easy I did it?"

John laughed and threw up his hands. "Whoa, there, partner," he said. "I give up. I didn't mean the work was easy. I meant you didn't walk away from it, that's all."

"Don't think there haven't been times when I wanted to," Cap said.

By now they were standing in front of the general store.

"You buy from Mr. Dunne?" Slocum asked.

"Dunne's all right. The only problem with him is he tries so hard to please ever'body, he don't please nobody," Cap said. "But he's got the only general store in these parts, so I have to do my buyin' from him."

"What kind of supplies will we be picking up?" John asked.

"Grub, of course," Cap said. "And ammunition.

Plenty of ammunition. We're going to be needing it, because there won't be any more men coming."

"I see," John asked. "How many have you got left?" he asked cautiously.

"Do you mean workin' men, or fightin' men?"

"Fightin' men," John said.

Cap cleared his throat. "One," he said. "That is, besides you and me. There's three of us all told."

"You've only got one more man riding with you?"

"That's about the size of it."

"Hope it's a good man."

"Well, Mindy's a pretty fair shot."

"Mindy? That an Indian name?"

"Girl's name. Mindy's my daughter."

"Oh, shit," John said.

4

At first the girl standing in the hayloft of the barn thought that one of the two riders might be her father. But she could tell, even from this distance, that neither of the riders sat the saddle like her father, nor did they sit like any of the line riders who worked for them. Whoever these two men were, Mindy Locke knew they hadn't been invited.

Mindy pushed a couple of bales of hay in front of the window, then lay down on the loft and sighted her Henry rifle toward the intruders. She kept them in sight until they rode all the way in, passed the gate, and went up to the corral fence. They stopped at the gate and looked around cautiously.

"You sure he ain't here?" one of the riders said to the other.

"This here's Tuesday, ain't it? He always goes into town on Tuesday."

"What if he ain't left yet?"

"He's left. If he hadn't left, you think we would'a got this far?"

"What do you aim to do?"

"I aim to torch the house," the first rider said. He chuckled. "That ought to give him a nice surprise when he comes back."

"You two men just turn around and get out of here!" Mindy called.

"What? Who's that? Who are you?"

"Never mind who I am. Just get out of here," Mindy called again.

One of the riders laughed. "It's a girl. Where are you, honey? I'd like to see what you look like."

"This is your last warning!" Mindy called.

"Sounds like she's in the barn," one of the men said.

The two riders started toward the barn. Mindy aimed at the hat of one of them, held her breath, and squeezed the trigger. The gun roared back against her shoulder and the rider's hat flew off.

"Hey! What the hell? You could've killed me, you crazy little bitch!"

"If you don't leave now, I *will* kill you," Mindy said.

"To hell with that!" the hatless rider said. He pulled his pistol and snapped several shots off toward the loft window of the barn. The bullets whistled overhead, and Mindy returned fire. She hit one of the riders in the cheek of his ass, and heard him yell in pain.

"I'm gettin' out of here!" the wounded rider yelled. "That crazy bitch is gonna kill us both!"

When the rider who was hit in the butt started to leave, the hatless rider lost his own courage and followed behind. Mindy threw another couple of shots after them. Then, when she was satisfied they were completely gone, she sat down on the bale of hay and began to tremble. Then hysteria took over, and she began to laugh. It wasn't the best shot she had ever made, but it would give the man something to think about every time he sat down.

"I call her the Lazy L," Cap Locke said as they rode out to his ranch. He chuckled. "Shows how much I knew about it when I started in. I figured all I'd have to do is turn a few cows loose, let 'em feed and water, then sell 'em off. Nothin' for me to do but lay around while they fatten up. That's why I named it the Lazy L."

John laughed. "So you were going to be lazy, huh?"

"That's what I thought. Only it didn't work out that way."

"I asked you about fighting men earlier. How about workers? You got any riders out?"

"A few. Some in the shacks, some making roundup in the breaks or the canyon. They're good men, John. Hard-workin', honest men. They aren't fighters, though, and I don't feel right 'bout askin' them to fight."

"Some of them may get forced into it, whether they want to or not," John suggested.

"Some of 'em already have. Two of 'em were hit

by half a dozen men off the Box S yesterday."

"Box S? You mean they were Tucker Scarns's hands?"

"Yeah. Gunhands. The riders that hit my boys weren't workin' men, I can guarantee you that. Fact is, I doubt that any of 'em ever held a brandin' iron in their life, 'less it was a runnin' iron for changin' brands."

"Does Scarns have any honest men working for him?"

"He had a few," Cap said. "Most of them has done left. Some come to work for me, the rest lit out for other territory. Mostly what he has now are gunfighters, as my boys found out yesterday up at the water hole."

"What happened?"

"Well, I got me a real good way of waterin' my stock. See, what I done was kind of connect all the low spots together, and that lets water flow natural like from the Red River. The stock that's up in the breaks, though, don't always have water, so my riders got to bring them down now and again. Yesterday two of my boys, Lonnie Gaskins and Earl Kimmson are their names, brought a few head down from the breaks, like I said. They was watering the stock when half a dozen of Scarns's gunnies come swoopin' down on 'em, whoopin', hollerin', blazin' away."

"Gaskins and Kimmson. Were they armed?"

"Oh, they was both heeled, all right. Hell, ever' cowboy I got is packin' iron now, even though they ain't none of 'em ever shot at anythin' more dangerous than a rattler . . . and most of them can't hit that."

"Did they return fire?"

"Yeah, they managed to shoot back. Fact is, all my men have been willin' to return fire if it ain't no more than an occasional potshot bein' took at 'em. But this business yesterday, John, that was a lot more than a little potshot. It was an outright attack."

"Were your men hit?"

"Yeah, both of 'em was shot up pretty bad. Young Lonnie Gaskins now, I figure he's gonna pull through. But the other fella, Earl Kimmson, I don't know. It's touch and go at best."

"Where are they now?"

"I got 'em back at the place. Mindy's moved them outa the bunkhouse into the big house. She's takin' care of 'em best she can."

"I meant to ask you about Mindy a while ago."

"She's been a real big help to me, John. Fact is, I don't know what I would'a done without her."

"You've got her tendin' your hands, you said yourself she was manning a rifle. That's a pretty tall order for a little girl."

Cap smiled. "Little girl?"

"Well, isn't she?"

"She's not too big," Cap agreed, but that was all he said.

"Nevertheless, it sounds like you got about as much as you can handle, old friend."

"I'm afraid so. If it gets too much more serious, I might have to pull out."

"Damn, Cap, how much more serious can it get?" John asked. "None of your men are fighters, there's just the two of us . . ."

"Three," Cap put in quickly. "Don't forget Mindy."

"All right, let's say Mindy can hold her own. That

still just leaves the three of us. And from what I hear in town, Scarns damn near has an army. Plus, he has Preacher Jack."

Cap chuckled. "You're a pretty good poker player, as I recall."

"I do all right," John said.

"You know that a smart poker player don't show all his cards at one time. Could be I've got me an ace or two, face down, myself."

"What are you talking about?"

"John, you recollect the time you 'n' me 'n' near a dozen of Quantrill's best had to take that little ol' farmhouse near Fletcher's Mill? We figured we'd ride right in there and rout those Yankees easy, but it took us all day. Fact is, we never would've took it at all if you hadn't snuck around to the rear. Then, when we got the house, we found out they was no more 'n half a dozen Yankees been holdin' us off all that time."

John chuckled. "Yeah, I remember. But if I recall, they had a little help that day in the form of a Whitworth six-pounder."

"You remember anything about that gun?"

"Sure. It's a breech-loading, rifled piece of field artillery. A pretty wicked piece of business, if I recall."

"It'll throw a six-pound projectile better than a mile," Cap said proudly. "And it has a bursting radius of five yards."

"Don't remind me. I remember it well," John said.

"What do you think would've happened that day if you hadn't managed to get around behind them?"

"I don't know. We would've either taken a lot of

casualties, or we would've passed the house by."

"If we had passed them by, they would've been right there waitin' for ol' Jeff Thompson when he come along," Cap said. "General Thompson told me hisself that you saved the day for us. Remember? He come ridin' in on that white horse of his, that big green feather stickin' up outa his hat. Oh, he was a dandy." Cap chuckled.

"Why are you bringing all that up now, Cap? What's that got to do with this?"

"Just this: I don't figure Scarns has got a John Slocum ridin' for him. No, nor anyone close to it. I don't think he'll be able to get around behind us, and when they come, we'll have our little surprise laid in and waitin' for 'em. We're gonna blow 'em right to hell, and I don't think his men are gonna be willin' to take that many casualties."

John looked over at Cap. "My God, Cap, you telling me you have a cannon out at your place?"

"Not just a cannon, John, my boy. I've got a Whitworth six-pounder, the sweetest piece you ever saw, just like the one we had to face at Fletcher's Mill," Cap said.

"Does it work?"

"She's in perfect condition," Cap insisted. "Not only that, but I've got all the shells, powder, and primer we could possibly need. Fact is, the bulk of the supplies I just bought in town are powder, lead, dynamite, caps, and fuses. Plus, I got lots of rifle and pistol ammunition. I promise you, John, if Scarns is aimin' to fight a war, then I plan on givin' him a lot more than he ever bargained for."

"I'll admit that gives you an edge Scarns probably

isn't counting on," John said. "Even so, with the number of men he has riding for him, it's going to have to be a defensive war."

"Yeah, but wait'll you see our defenses, John. You'll be proud of me."

"That's just the first damned thing I want to see," Slocum replied.

It wasn't the first thing he saw. The first thing he saw was a slender rider who galloped out from the house to meet them as they came up the road. The rider and the horse were one, a graceful combination of muscle and bone, grace and skill. Then, as the rider drew up even with them, John saw that it was a girl, all freckles and cowlick, denim pants, and her daddy's shirt. She looked like a kid as she brushed her blond hair back from her forehead. Her eyes sparkled like the sun bouncing off water, and she smiled broadly at John.

"You must be the John Slocum Pa has been tellin' me about. I figured you'd be three times bigger than you are."

"Three times bigger?"

"You'd near have to be to live up to the giant my pa's made you out to be," the girl said with a good-natured laugh. She stuck her hand out. "I'm Mindy Locke."

Mindy was wearing a Starr pistol, and she had a Henry carbine thrown across her saddle. There was a smell of black powder about her, and a little smudge of black on her cheek.

"Mindy, what happened? Any trouble?" Cap said. "How come you got black powder smeared acrost your face? You been shootin' at somethin'?"

"You doggone right I've been shooting at something," Mindy answered proudly. "A couple of galoots rode in, nosing around, trying to see what
they could turn up. They won't be so quick to come
back. I winged one of them, knocked the hat off the
other."

"Where were you?" Cap asked.

"I was on lookout in the hayloft," Mindy said,
pointing back to the barn. She laughed, and her
laugh was bouncy and energetic, like the bubbling of
a mountain stream. "Aren't you gonna ask me where
I winged him?"

"I figure you're gonna tell me," Cap said.

"Not exactly, because I'm a lady and it's too deli-
cate to mention with a gentleman present," Mindy
said. "But I'll give you a hint. The fella I hit was
standin' in his stirrups when the two of 'em rode out
of here."

Cap and John laughed.

"Where are the others?" Mindy asked. "Are they
comin' later?"

"What others?"

"I thought you were going to pick up three men,
three gunfighters. Didn't they show?"

"They showed, all right," Cap said. "They
showed yesterday, and one of Scarns's men put them
in the ground."

"One man? One man killed all three?"

"Yep."

Mindy shuddered. "I don't ever want to run across
that man."

"You won't," Cap said. He nodded toward John.

"John's already faced him down, sent him to his maker."

Mindy's eyes grew wide with awe, and just a little fear, as she looked at John.

"You . . . you killed him?"

"It seemed to be the thing to do at the moment," John said.

"You must be awfully fast," she suggested.

"I've managed to stay alive," John said without elaboration.

"Well, come on, John, I'll take you up to the house, show you your room, then we'll eat supper. You must be hungry," Cap said.

"Starved," John agreed.

"You got anything cookin', daughter?"

"Made a stew," Mindy said. "It was the best I could do, what with standin' lookout too."

"Stew sounds just fine," John said.

Slocum looked at the house as they approached. It was made of mail-order lumber and heavy timbers. The windows were all boarded up, with gun ports. The shutters were thick oak, hard as concrete, aged in the Texas sun and wind.

John got a good sample of the wind a little while later when he came out onto the porch to wash his face and hands for supper. The wind was blowing about fifty miles an hour. There were a few shirts and a couple of pants hanging on the clothesline, and they were standing straight out. John saw Cap walking back from the barn. He was leaning into the blowing wind to keep his balance.

"The wind always blow like this?" John asked.

"Not always," Cap answered, holding his hat on his head. "Some days it blows real hard. Mindy's got supper set. You 'bout ready?"

"I got a whiff of it a few minutes ago," John said. "If I didn't have an appetite before, I sure do now."

"Let's get to it," Cap said.

5

The young lady who set the supper table was nothing at all like the tomboy who had come riding out to meet them. This lady was dressed in a slim-waisted gingham dress, had her blond hair tamed and curled at the ends, and moved about in a fragrance of lilac.

And yet, it was the same person, as was obvious when she smiled at John, showing the same perfectly formed white teeth and gleaming eyes.

"Well, now, will you look at my daughter?" Cap said. "If I didn't know any better, I'd say she got all dressed up there to set her cap for you, John. You'd better keep an eye on her."

"Pa!" Mindy said sharply, and her cheeks flamed with color. Nevertheless, there was a light shining deep in her eyes, and it didn't come from the lantern's reflection. John suddenly realized that there was a degree of truth in Cap's jest. Mindy was as cute as a bug's ear, but she was obviously man-hunting.

Cap laughed. "John asked me if you wasn't a just a little girl. I told him you wasn't too big."

"I have to admit," John said, "you aren't at all what I expected."

"I hope you aren't disappointed," Mindy said.

John smiled. "I reckon not much."

John cleaned his plate and Mindy, without asking, jumped up to refill it. He thanked her, but his enjoyment of her cooking seemed thanks enough.

"Well, John, if you can pull yourself away from the dinner table," Cap said, "what say we have coffee and a smoke on the front porch? The sun's down, the wind's died off; we can talk out there."

"Sounds fine to me," John said.

"Oh, honey, how are the two boys?" Cap asked. "Lonnie and Earl?"

"I made a little clear broth for them," Mindy said. "I thought I'd see if I can get them to take it."

"Sounds like a good idea," Cap agreed.

Outside, the dark sky stretched overhead like the vaulted ceiling of a great cathedral. Except for the tiny glimmers of thousands of stars, the sky was forebodingly silent and empty.

John walked out to the edge of the porch and looked up at the night sky. The stars ranged from the very brightest, which were white and blinking almost like beacons, to the dimmest, which were no more than a suggestion of stardust shimmering mysteriously in the trackless distance.

"Big country, ain't it?" Cap said beside him. Cap

lit his smoke and his face glowed yellow in the flare of the match. He held the burning lucifer over to John and John put the end of his cigar to the flame, then drew until it was lit. Cap blew the match out and flipped it into the night.

"Pretty big," John agreed.

"I figured it was big enough," Cap said. He sighed. "I come out here after the War, wantin' to forget things I had seen . . . things I had done."

"I reckon we all wanted to do that," John said. "Different ones of us chose different ways to do it, that's all."

"Yeah, well, I wanted to make a home for my family. I thought sure this country was big enough to let a man settle down in peace. Hell, when I got here my nearest neighbor was fifty miles away. Now I'm havin' to fight just to hold on to what I got."

"It looks to me like it's worth fightin' for," John said.

"Yeah, I guess it is at that," Cap said. He belched, then rubbed his stomach. "How'd you like the stew?"

John smiled. "Couldn't you tell by the way I ate?"

"I got to hand it to Mindy. She's gettin' to be a pretty good cook. She never had to before. We always had us a belly robber on the place. But Cookie left when the shootin' first started. Said he fought at Shiloh, he'd seen enough fightin' for one life." Cap was silent for a moment. "Can't say as I blame him none."

"Was he a good cook?"

"Pretty good. He made the heaviest biscuits in the world, but he knew how to work beef to make it some tender. Most cooks fry it till it's hard as shoe leather. Hell, you 'member the fella we had cookin' for us when we rode with Quantrill?''

John laughed. "We used to say if we could get him to join the Yankees the War would be over in six weeks, they'd all die of poisonin'."

"He was pretty awful," Cap agreed.

The door opened behind them, and John caught the scent of lilacs. A light step crossed the porch.

"How are the boys doin'?" Cap asked.

"Lonnie's doing better. He ate some broth," Mindy said. "But, Pa, Earl doesn't look very good. I think you ought to take a look."

"I don't know what I can do," Cap started. He looked over at John. "But I recollect you've done some doctorin', John. Why don't you look in on them with me?"

"Be glad to," John agreed.

Both men were in the same room, in the same bed. The room was small, and it smelled of kerosene from the lantern which burned yellow on the bedside table. The wallpaper was buff-colored, with a pattern of baskets of blue flowers. The window was open about six inches and a gentle breeze drifted through. Frogs and crickets serenaded from the dark outside.

Earl was semi-conscious and delirious. His head was rolling from side to side and his lips were moving, though he was too weak to be talking loud enough for anyone to hear.

"Poor Earl," Lonnie said. "He was callin' for his mama a while ago."

Lonnie was pale as a sheet. Earl was just a kid, about eighteen, younger even than Mindy. Lonnie was a little older, more Mindy's age.

"Mindy said you took a little broth," Cap said.

"Yes, sir. It was real tasty; Mindy's treatin' us real

good," Lonnie said. Lonnie looked at John and his eyes wrinkled in curiosity.

"Lonnie, this is John Slocum, a friend of mine," Cap said.

Lonnie smiled. "John Slocum? I've heard of you," he said. "They say you're pretty fast. You here to help us?"

"I'll do what I can do," John said.

Lonnie smiled again. "From what I hear, that's a goodly amount. Wait till I get on my feet again, Mr. Slocum. I'd like a second chance at the men who did this to Earl 'n' me."

The kid's got gumption, John thought. *He won't run away.*

"Let me take a look at your wounds," John said.

"He's shot clean through the calf of one leg," Cap said. "It's swelled up like a balloon."

John pulled the cover to one side and looked at the bullet hole.

"What do you think?" Lonnie asked. "You reckon I'm gonna lose the leg?"

"What makes you think that?" John asked.

"I've read about war wounds," Lonnie explained. "I know how a bullet wound in the leg nearly always meant the doctor had to take it off."

"We've come some ways since then," John said. "Someone's been takin' real good care of your wound. It's clean, no sign of gangrene."

"It's Mindy what's been keepin' it clean," Lonnie said.

"And it was pure luck the bullet passed all the way through," Cap added. "We didn't have to dig around for it. But Earl was gut-shot. It's considerable worse."

John covered Lonnie's leg, then pulled the cover down to look at Earl's wounds. Earl had two bullet holes in the trunk of his body, one very close to a lung, and another that might have torn up his spleen. John put his hand on Earl's forehead. He was burning up with fever.

"How is he, Mr. Slocum?" Lonnie asked anxiously.

"I won't lie to you, Lonnie," John said. "He's not in very good shape."

John pulled the cover back over Earl, then left the room. Cap walked out with him.

"Think he'll make it?" Cap asked when they returned to the front porch.

"Tomorrow night will tell the tale," John answered. "He's good until morning. Fever burns up a lot of poison."

"Scarns may think it's all a question of land and water rights," Cap said angrily. "But it ain't. It's a hell of a lot more'n that. It's a question of whether or not men, good, decent, honest, hard-workin' men like Lonnie and Earl, can earn themselves a livin' by cowboyin'. And it's a question of murder."

"Cap, you ever know this Tucker Scarns before?"

"Ran acrost him a few times higher up in the Panhandle, over along the Smoky Hill. Always thought he was a bad one who'd never amount to much. But he run into some luck a few months back, I reckon. Used to ride with Chisholm. Then somehow he come up with enough money to buy his own spread."

"The hell you say," Slocum said, and he chewed on that without saying anything more.

• • •

The bed in John's room was large and inviting. Mindy had already been in here; the cover was turned down and the pillows fluffed. That wasn't the only reason he knew she had been here, though. Her scent hung in the air like a signature. A coal-oil lamp sat on the bedside table. John lit it, but kept the flame low. It needed only the twist of the wick key to flood the room with bright light.

If need be, John could make himself comfortable with a saddle blanket and a poncho. He considered it luxury when he had a dry spot and a bedroll. Those times when he could enjoy a bed, clean sheets, and a pillow were treats to be savored, so he was looking forward to this night's sleep.

John left the lamp low, undressed in the semi-darkness, and slipped in between the cool sheets. He turned the key to snuff the flame entirely and sleep was upon him within a matter of minutes.

He had no idea how long he had been asleep when something awakened him. He opened his eyes abruptly, his senses attuned to whatever had disturbed him.

"Mr. Slocum? Mr. Slocum, are you awake?"

John smiled and relaxed. Mindy was just outside his door. He lit the lantern again and the room was bathed in a soft, golden glow.

"Come in, Mindy," he said.

The door opened and Mindy stepped inside, then pushed the door closed behind her. She stood there for a moment, bathed golden in the wavering flame.

"I . . . I hope you don't mind the intrusion," she said. "I can't sleep. I want to talk a while."

"Be my guest," John said. He sat up in bed and

the cover slipped down to his waist, baring his shoulders and chest. Mindy looked at his naked torso and took in a sharp, rasping breath, though she tried hard to control it.

"May I sit here, on the edge of the bed?" she asked, crossing the room and sitting down before he answered.

In this position she was silhouetted by the lamplight and though her nightgown wasn't designed to be sheer, it was so thin and threadbare that it was translucent. John could see no detail, such as the flesh tone of her skin, but he could clearly see the outline of her lithe, young body. The breasts, hard and firm, the nipples tightly drawn, the flatness of her stomach, then the flare of her hips provided intriguing shadows for him to enjoy.

John was experiencing a light, giddy feeling, and for a moment he wasn't sure what it was. Then he realized exactly what it was. He wanted this woman. He wanted to make love to her.

No, he thought. *She isn't a woman, she's just a little girl, Cap's daughter.* How could he be thinking such thoughts about her? But even as he tried to push the thoughts away, she touched a scar on his shoulder and her touch ignited a fire which burned all the way to his loins.

"Oh," she said. "How did you get that?"

"A little girl bit me," John teased.

"Really? How old was she?"

"About your age," John answered, trying to keep a proper perspective on things.

"I'm not a little girl," Mindy insisted. She turned, and though it wasn't a studied move, the turn brought her nightgown tight against her breast and her nipple stuck out in a tight little point. A little vein on her neck fluttered. Her lips were full and inviting.

As John looked at her he sighed. It wasn't working. No matter how hard he tried, he couldn't see her as a little girl. He could only see her as a desirable young woman. "No, I guess you aren't a little girl at that," he agreed.

"I'm already older than my mother was when I was born."

"She was as pretty as you, too," John said.

Mindy's eyes lit up brightly. "Oh! Did you know my mother?"

"Sure," John said. "She was the prettiest girl in Sage County. Half the men in the state were camping around her pa's farm, but Cap was the one she chose."

"She was pretty, wasn't she?" Mindy said. She sighed. "I miss her terribly."

"Cap said she died two years ago?"

"It came on sudden," Mindy said. "She got a chill, then a high fever, and within a few days she was dead." A tear came to Mindy's eyes, and John reached up to brush it away gently.

"Life out here is hard for everyone," John said. "Sometimes it's particularly hard on women. I'm not sure I know why.

"Maybe that's why she wanted me to leave," Mindy said.

"What do you mean?"

"When I was a little girl she used to tell me about the plans she had for me. I was going to go back East, attend a boarding school somewhere, maybe in St. Louis or Cincinnati or someplace like that. Then I was going to meet a fine young gentleman and live in an elegant house in a city."

"Is that what you want to do?"

"I guess so."

"Really? Or is that what you want to do because that's what your mother wanted?"

"Well, I want to please her," Mindy said.

"Maybe your mother wanted that for you because she thought it would please you," John suggested. "I knew Earline pretty well, and I'm sure that she would be happy with anything that makes you happy."

"Maybe you're right," Mindy said.

"So, what would make you happy? What would you like to do?"

Mindy smiled broadly. "I'd like to stay right here," she said. "I'd like to stay right here on the Lazy L and make it into one of the best ranches in Texas."

"Well, from what I've seen of it, I'd say you and your pa have made a pretty good start," John suggested.

"We'll do it too, if Scarns and those scoundrels who work for him will let us," Mindy said. She put her fingers on John's jawline, felt a muscle twitch just under her fingertips. "With you here, we can't lose," she said.

"You may be counting on more than I can deliver," John suggested.

"No, I don't think so," Mindy said. She leaned toward him and he could feel her breasts beneath her thin gown, her hot breath on his cheek. "I think you could deliver anything," she said.

As she spoke her lips were just a breath away, and she concluded her statement by kissing him full on the mouth. Gently but forcefully, John put his hands on Mindy's shoulders and pushed her away.

"I think we'd better get some sleep now," he said. "It looks like we've got our work cut out for us on this place."

"Why, John Slocum," Mindy teased in a voice which seemed older than her years, "I thought you weren't afraid of anything."

"Good night, Mindy."

Mindy stood up and looked down at John for a long moment. Her eyes seemed to shine with an inner light. A knowing smile played across her mouth. She turned in such a way as to beautifully accent the lines of her body, and though it was subtle, John wasn't sure it was an accident.

"Good night, John Slocum," she said. She leaned down to twist the key on the lamp and the flame was snuffed. "Pleasant dreams," she added.

A moment later she was gone, with only the haunting scent of her to speak of her presence.

6

The slanting bars of the brightly shining moon fell through the window onto Mindy's bed. Had John looked in at her then, any lingering thought of her being a little girl would have been totally dispelled.

It wasn't a little girl at all, but a beautiful young woman who lay on the bed, her blond hair fanned out upon the pillow in such a way as to frame her face with beauty. Her eyes were closed in sleep and no artist could have painted a more tranquil scene.

The scene may have been tranquil, but the sleep was fitful.

Mindy was bothered by a dream. There was an uneasiness, a sense of displacement that disquieted her. She turned in her bed to will the dream away, and the sudden movement awakened her. She lay in bed for a moment, trapped between wakefulness and sleep, wondering why she was so uneasy.

Then she remembered the dream, but when she tried to recall the details it slipped away into the shadowed recesses of her mind.

Now Mindy was fully awake, and she turned and fluffed her pillow and looked at the wall where the bright moonlight created a magic lantern show by projecting shadows formed by the trees and curtains. From the corral she heard a horse whicker, and she got out of bed and crossed over to the window to look outside.

Mindy felt a strange heat in her body, and she opened the window sash a bit to allow the breeze to cool her. She was puzzled by the heat, then the details of the dream which had slipped away a few moments earlier returned and it was no longer a mystery. She knew her feelings now for just what they were. They were the stirrings of sexual desire.

It wasn't fair, she thought. She was a full-grown woman, taking on the responsibilities of a full-grown woman, yet she had never experienced love. What if she died tomorrow? What if she got killed in this range war? She would go to her grave never knowing what it was like to have a man make love to her.

When Mindy had gone into John's room earlier, it had been to tell him how glad she was that he had come to help. But, deep down inside, Mindy hoped that John would take the initiative to make love to her. Despite her wishes and her strongest efforts to entice him, he had remained a perfect gentleman. She had had to complete the scenario in her dream.

Now that she was awake again, she knew that the dream was a poor substitute for the real thing. She was ready to take the irrevocable step that would take her, forever, across the line from girlhood to womanhood. More than she had ever wanted anything in her life, she wanted John Slocum to make love to her.

Suddenly Mindy smiled, recalling a favorite expression of her father's. If at first you don't succeed, try, try again. She doubted if he would approve of this particular application of his advice, but she was going to do it.

When Mindy came into John's room the second time, he wasn't surprised by it. He had been expecting her from the moment she left. Without a word to him, she stood just inside his door and removed her nightgown. In the silver splash of moonlight he could see her naked young body, the breasts uplifted and proud, the thighs shaded and inviting.

"Hello, Mindy," John said, displaying no shock at seeing her.

"You knew I would come," Mindy said.

"Yes."

"How did you know?"

"Some things, a man just knows."

"I'm frightened," Mindy said, and John knew that she wasn't frightened by the range war, but frightened by what she was feeling . . . what she was doing.

Mindy might have been frightened, but more than fear, she was experiencing want, and more than caution, she knew desire.

"Are you . . . are you going to send me away again?" Mindy asked.

"Mindy, are you sure you want to do this?" John asked.

"Yes, I'm very sure," Mindy answered. "John,

I'm almost twenty. I . . . I may never be loved, I may never have anyone to love. I can face the idea of dying, but I can't face the idea of never knowing what it was like to be a woman."

John pushed aside the top sheet of his bed, inviting her in. She smiled broadly, triumphantly, then slipped happily into bed beside him. John could feel her body trembling. He knew it wasn't from the cold.

As Mindy had never been with a man before, her erotic dream had been inadequate to the task of preparing her for what it was really like. The feel of John's smooth skin, rippling muscles, and obvious maleness aroused her to even greater heights of passion. Her hands moved of their own volition, tracing a path across his skin. She sucked in a little gasp of breath as she felt his erection for the first time, feeling its incredible heat, its throbbing power.

When John felt her long, cool fingers closing around his erection, a web of flame shot through his body. His fingers went to her thighs, slipped through the hair, and spread the moist lips. She was wet and hot and moaning with desire.

John moved over her then and Mindy, though inexperienced, knew through some innate instinct to raise her legs and spread her knees for him. She put her hand on his penis again and guided it into position, taking it into her slowly until it would go no farther, stopped by her intact maidenhead.

"No," she gasped. "Don't stop. Don't stop now, go on through, please, John, go on through."

John pushed through the little membrane of skin, felt her gasp with a sudden, unexpected pain, then felt her relax as the pain passed away to be replaced by sensations of pleasure.

John began thrusting and she raised her hips to meet him, taking him down inside her, sliding him across every nerve ending within. Mindy gasped with the pleasure of it, and cried with the joy of it as she built toward fulfillment. To John, it was as if Mindy's senses were like a restless willow in a windstorm, moving, tightening, latent with the promise of more.

He felt her when she orgasmed. Unable to hold back her cries of joy, moans of pleasure escaped her lips and she threw her arms around John and pulled him to her. John felt himself coming and he pumped harder, deeper, and faster.

Through the rest of the long night they stayed together, sometimes sleeping in each other's arms, sometimes exploring new avenues of pleasure, as the mutual lonesomeness was soaked up by their passion.

Much later, as they lay together, the sky paling in the east, Mindy sighed contentedly.

"Thank you for this night, John Slocum," she said.

Slocum squeezed her gently, but said nothing.

Mindy sat up. The nudity which was only suggested in the moonlight was now more visible in the gray light of morning. Somehow she looked more womanly this morning. She leaned over to kiss him, and a breast swung forward to brush against his arm. The nipple hardened at the contact, and John reached up to touch it.

"Don't get me aroused again," she said. "It is hard

enough for me to leave. You'll only make it more difficult."

"Are you leaving now?"

"Yes. My father gets up with the sun."

"I remember," John said.

"Then you know I must go."

John folded his hands behind his head and looked at her. He knew she was right. It would be very awkward if Cap found them together. But it was as difficult a moment for him as it was for her. Despite that, he smiled at her.

"Go," he said. "Go now, before I change my mind and keep you here by force."

Mindy smiled at him. "Why couldn't you have said that the first time I was in here?"

"What?"

"Never mind," she said. "It's just a private thought, that's all." Mindy walked over to the door, stood there in the early morning light, blew him a kiss, then stepped through the door. John thought of her running down the hall to her own room, totally naked. If anyone happened to be up at this hour they would be in for a strange sight.

John closed his eyes. Despite the fact that he had gotten very little sleep last night, he felt strangely rested.

The rider was dressed all in black. His real name was Jack Hawthorne, but he'd answered to the name of Preacher Jack for so long now that most people didn't know his real name.

He'd heard from Luke Hamrick and Bill Newcastle that John Slocum had arrived to ride for Cap Locke. Preacher Jack knew of John Slocum, knew that he was more than an ordinary gunhand. He knew too that he would probably have to face him before this was over.

It would be best if he could shoot him down early, kill him now and take all the fight out of Cap Locke. What better way than to put him to the adobe wall this very morning. Maybe get him when he stepped out to take a leak.

Preacher Jack saw the back door open, saw someone start toward the pump by the watering trough. At first he thought it might be Slocum, and he felt a sense of excitement as he snaked the Sharps from his saddle holster, then got into position behind a rock.

It wasn't Slocum. Whoever it was was barely able to walk. It occurred to Preacher Jack that it was probably one of the two riders he heard had been hit the day before yesterday. A couple of Scarns's men had come back to the Box S claiming they'd jumped two of Locke's cowboys at a watering hole. They hadn't killed them, but they shot them up pretty bad.

Preacher Jack spat a chew of tobacco out and watched the man as he staggered to the pump. He looked like he was pretty badly hurt. It'd probably be an act of Christian kindness to just go ahead and put this fella out of his misery.

Quietly, Preacher Jack quoted from Psalms: "Let the praises of God be in their throat and a two-edged sword in their hand; to wreak vengeance of the nations and punishment on the peoples."

He put the front sight on the head of the man at the pump, let out half a breath, then squeezed the trigger.

7

Cap was bright-eyed and eager for the new day. He wolfed down his eggs and potatoes and drank several cups of coffee as he made plans with John. John was responsive, but Mindy was rather subdued.

"What's the matter, girl, didn't you sleep well last night?" Cap asked.

Mindy smiled in embarrassment, and her cheeks flamed red. She looked at John as if they had been caught, and John saw a look of hunger deep in her eyes. He, too, had been remembering their night together, and wondered for a moment if that hunger was reflected in his own eyes.

"I had a . . . a wonderful night," she said. "Why do you ask?"

"Well, hell, girl, you ain't said ten words since we

sat down to breakfast," Cap complained. "I just thought . . ."

Cap's words were interrupted sharply by the booming explosion of a heavy-caliber rifle shot.

"My God!" Cap shouted. "They're here! Get movin', girl!"

Cap sprang to the back door. Mindy, grabbing the Henry which was never far from her side, was right behind her father. John, still unaccustomed to his surroundings, was left to lumber after them.

They found Lonnie weeping, holding his face in his hands, sitting on the porch of the bunkhouse.

"Lonnie, what is it?" Cap asked. "What happened here?"

"It's Earl," Lonnie said. "He got up this mornin' and went outside. I mean he just got up, without so much as a word, and started walkin'. I called to him. I said, 'Earl, what are you doin'? You'd best get back in bed.' But he never answered, he just kept on walkin'."

"Must have been delirious," John suggested.

"He come outside, and I seen him staggerin' toward the waterin' trough. I started after him. Then the shot just boomed. I ran over here to the bunkhouse out of the line of fire, but Earl, he . . ." Lonnie stopped and took a deep breath. "God damn them, they never gave Earl a chance. They shot him in the head and he probably was goin' to die anyway."

"Stay with him, Mindy," John said.

"Where you going?" Cap wanted to know.

"I'm going to have a look at Earl."

John started toward the watering trough and Cap trailed after him. They saw the boy lying face down, his feet turned out, palms facing up, his body twisted at cockeyed angles. It wasn't the way a body lay unless it was dead.

"Son of a bitch," Cap breathed. "Look at that."

John looked around, trying to determine where the shot had come from. He had the uneasy feeling that someone was watching them.

He spotted the early morning sunlight glinting off a rifle barrel from behind a distant clump of sage. He reacted quicker than thought. "Cap, get down," he whispered, pushing him down just as the sound of the rifle report reached them. It was a deep, barking sound, the same big-caliber gun they had heard earlier. Sharps, most likely, John thought.

The heavy round chunked through the top edge of the water trough, kicked up dirt a few feet beyond, then whistled on out into the valley. If John hadn't reacted at precisely the moment he did, Cap would have been hit.

"Reckon I owe you one," Cap said.

John and Cap moved in tight behind the water trough. It gave them a position of cover, but without rifles they were incapable of returning fire.

A second round screamed by, hitting the dirt so close to John's face that his face was peppered with stinging sand. The heavy report floated just behind the bullet. Whoever was shooting at them was an expert marksman.

"Stay down!" Mindy called. "I see where he is!"

John heard the bark of Mindy's Henry and he saw a puff of dust just below where he had seen the smoke from the Sharps. Cap was right about one thing. Mindy was an expert marksman. She had zeroed in on the sniper with her very first shot. She fired a second round, but by now it was obvious to John that the sniper had moved.

"We can't go on like this," John said. "Those bastards can come in here any time they want and pick us off one by one, just like they did Earl."

"I know. When it quiets down, I'll show you the setup. Thanks again, friend, for shoving me out of the way of that fifty-caliber pellet."

They heard retreating hoofbeats then, and knew that the sniper was on his way out. They also knew their man would be back, maybe with help next time.

"We need to get Earl in the ground," John said, standing and looking down at the young cowboy.

"Yeah," Cap agreed. "I'll get a couple of shovels from the barn. Mindy can cover us."

"All I can say is, it's a hell of an end for a kid who didn't expect to do any more than tend a few cows," Cap said as they smoothed the mound of Earl's grave. "We couldn't even give the boy a funeral."

"A funeral wouldn't make him any less dead," John said. "And it doesn't make his friends miss him any more. I reckon Earl understands."

"Yeah," Cap agreed. "I guess so. Come on, I told you I would show you around the place, and that's just what I aim to do. I think you'll see that Scarns hasn't picked an amateur to play war with. If that son of a bitch wants me he's gonna have to come get me, and I sure as hell don't intend to make it easy for him."

John followed Cap around the spread and saw that Cap had really done his preparation. Cap was right. If Tucker Scarns planned to take the Lazy L, he was going to have to work for it.

Cap showed John thick log barriers he had constructed, mounded over with dirt and clumps of sage so that they were invisible until a man walked right up on them.

"But that ain't the best of it," Cap said. "Wait till you see what I got up here."

On the highest point of the ground, behind the log barriers, Cap had set up his six-pounder, a breech-loading Whitworth, all camouflaged, with a good supply of shell and powder. In addition to the gun he had set up rifle bunkers with crossfire angles all laid out, so as to cover charges from any direction.

"What do you think?" Cap asked proudly.

John whistled softly and shook his head. "I think you've done one hell of a job laying out the defenses," he said. "What about the dynamite? What are your plans for it?"

"Glad you asked. You're the powder man. I remember what you did to that bridge down to Fayetteville. Thought maybe you'd come up with some sort of plan."

"You haven't done anything with it yet?"

"Nope. It's all yours," Cap promised.

"All right, I'll make a few welcoming preparations of my own," John said.

After a thorough tour of the defenses and the most probable approach paths by any attacking group of men, they walked back to the main house. There they found Lonnie sitting up at the kitchen table, drinking coffee with Mindy.

"You're looking a lot better than you did yesterday," John said.

"I'm feelin' some better," Lonnie admitted. "My leg's not throbbin' like it was, and I think the swelling's gone down."

"Good. Looks like you're recovering all right."

"I just wish I'd woke up in time to stop Earl."

"It's just one of those things, Lonnie," John said quietly. "We can't blame ourselves when things like that happen."

"What are we going to do, Mr. Slocum?" Lonnie asked.

John looked at Mindy and saw that she was asking the same question with her eyes. He smiled at her.

"Do?" he said. "Well, I plan to protect Cap's holdings and cattle here. That's what I plan to do."

"Good," Lonnie said resolutely. "I was hopin' you'd say that. If you'll have me, you can count on me to help."

"You think you can handle a rifle position?"

"Maybe not today," Lonnie admitted. "I'm still a little weak. But I'll be able to in a day or so."

"That ought to be good enough," John said. "I don't figure Scarns will try anything more than he tried this morning . . . at least, not for a day or so. But we have to let what happened to Earl be a warning to us. We can't go around without paying attention. The way it is now, they can sneak in a sniper just about any time and pick one of us off. We've got to keep our eyes and ears open."

"Wish we had us a couple of good dogs," Cap said.

"Maybe I can rig something up that'll work just as well," John suggested.

"You got somethin' in mind?" Cap asked.

"Yeah, maybe some way we can set up a warning system."

"How you gonna do that?" Lonnie asked.

"Mindy, what have you been doing with the tin cans after you empty them?"

"They're in a barrel out behind the kitchen," Mindy said. "Normally we bury them, but with all this going on, they've been piling up."

"Good," John said. "We can use them. You have twine?"

"Twine? No, I don't think so. I might find a ball of yarn."

"You don't need to do that," Lonnie said. "There's maybe three or four balls of twine out in the bunkhouse."

"What in the world is there so much twine out there for?" Cap asked.

Lonnie smiled sheepishly. "Me 'n' Earl was savin' it. We was gonna build a kite that would fly to the moon this summer."

John chuckled. "Tell me, Lonnie, do you think you could call off your moon flying long enough to let me use the string?"

"Sure," Lonnie said, his cheeks flaming in embarrassment. "It was mostly Earl's idea anyway."

"What are you going to do, John?" Mindy asked.

"Watch," John answered mysteriously. "Maybe you'll learn something."

Mindy followed John around as he worked. He ran a long line from each rifle position back to the house, then tied the line to a tin can.

"Now," he explained when he was finished. "Whoever is on watch can warn the rest of us just by pulling on the string. That way, even if we're in the house, we'll know when someone is coming. We'll even know which rifle position the warning is coming from, by whichever can is shaking. And whoever give us warning won't have to expose himself to Scarns's men.

"You're a genius!" Mindy exclaimed.

"Now for the dynamite charges," John said.

Slocum looked at the lay of the land. When he and Cap had walked around on their inspection tour earlier, he had figured the most likely approaches. Now he used that information to set dynamite charges in all the strategic locations.

Once the charges were planted, the next thing to do was to run long fuses from each charge to a secure position where they could be lit. He chose the rifle pit closest to the house, then doubled the fuses just to be safe. By the time he was finished working, he had established a system of land mines that would stop a charging army.

And he figured that was just what Scarns would throw at them.

8

Preacher Jack sat in the back of the saloon, nursing a drink and playing a game of "Old Sol." He would have welcomed a game of poker but since nearly everyone was afraid of him, it was hard to find people who would play with him. He counted out three cards but couldn't find a play. The second card down was a red nine and there was a black ten on the board. Preacher Jack played the red nine.

The batwing doors swung open and a cowboy came in and stepped up to the bar. He was a real cowhand, not a gunman, and he worked for Scarns.

"Tom, let me have a whiskey," he said. "Leave the bottle."

"Sure thing, Fred," Tom replied, sliding the bottle across to him. Fred put his money down on the bar and poured himself a drink. Then he turned and looked back toward Preacher Jack.

"Is it true?" he asked.

Preacher Jack continued to play his game.

"You, preacher man, whatever the hell they call you," Fred said, "I asked if it was true?"

Preacher Jack peered up at him through cold, lifeless eyes. "You talkin' to me?"

"Yeah, I'm talkin' to you," Fred said angrily. He poured himself another glass of whiskey and tossed it down. "I asked you if it was true?"

"I don't know what you're talkin' about," Preacher Jack said quietly.

"He don't know what I'm talkin' about," Fred mimicked. He looked squarely at Preacher Jack. "I hear you kilt Earl Kimmson this mornin'. Shot 'im right through the head, they say."

"What concern is it of yours?" Preacher Jack asked.

"Earl was a good man," Fred said. "Me 'n' him rode together some for Mr. Goodnight. He was a cowman, mister. A working cowhand. You know what that is?"

Preacher Jack went on with his game.

"I'm talkin' to you, mister!" Fred shouted.

Preacher Jack put down his cards and stared at Fred. The others in the saloon knew now that things had gone too far. They knew blood was about to be spilled and they began, slowly, quietly, to ease out of the way, leaving a clear line of fire between Preacher Jack and Fred.

"Fred, is it?" Preacher Jack asked quietly.

"Yeah, that's right. Fred Stone. I punch cows,

mister. I'm an honest hand, and I ain't workin' for Tucker Scarns no more. Not if he sees fit to hire the likes of you."

"Well, Fred, if that's the case, I think you might be wise to put that bottle down and go on outside, get up on your horse, and ride clear on out of Texas. Why don't you head up Wyoming way? I hear they punch lots of cows up there."

"Oh, I'll be leavin' in a minute," Fred said. "But when I do it ain't because you're tellin' me to go. And I ain't ridin' up to Wyoming. No, sir. I'm goin' out to the Lazy L, where a few good men are left. I figure they'll be needin' another hand since you murdered Earl this mornin'."

"In case you haven't heard," Preacher Jack said, "There's a range war goin' on right now. If anyone is killed during a range war it's not murder. It's an act of war."

"Call it what you want, mister. I call it murder," Fred said. "Tell me—you're supposed to be so good with a gun, why didn't you call out Cap Locke's new man?"

"You mean Slocum?" Preacher Jack asked. "It didn't seem appropriate."

Fred laughed bitterly. "Fancy talk for what's the real reason."

"What is the real reason?"

"You was scared," Fred said. "You're a yellow-belly coward who can only murder from behind a rock."

"I suppose you're ready to back those words up?" Preacher Jack said.

"I don't have to," Fred said. "I told you, I'm a

workin' hand, not a gunfighter. I'm not even packin' a gun. Course, I guess you could shoot me in the back if you wanted to."

"Give him a gun," Preacher Jack said coldly.

No one moved, and Preacher Jack saw Luke Hamrick standing at the end of the bar, just out of the line of fire.

"Give him your gun, Hamrick," Preacher Jack said.

"Aw, now, Preacher Jack, the boy's upset, that's all. Him and Earl was good friends, I used to see them in here together all the time. You don't want to fight him."

"Give him your gun or pull it and use it yourself," Preacher Jack said coldly. He turned three-quarters of the way toward Luke.

"Sure," Luke answered quickly. "Sure, if that's what you want, I'll be glad to give it to him." Luke took his gun out of his holster, then slid it down the bar to Fred.

"Pick it up," Preacher Jack said to Fred.

"You got your gun in a holster," Fred said. "That gives you an advantage."

"Pick the gun up and aim it at me," Preacher Jack said. "When you see me draw, pull the trigger."

Fred laughed. "Who are you kidding?"

"Pick it up or I'll shoot you down right now," Preacher Jack said. He grinned cruelly. "Here's your chance. You might get lucky. After all, you did say I was yellow, didn't you?"

Fred's hand started shaking, and he poured himself another glass of whiskey, then tossed the drink down. He set the empty glass on the bar.

"Let me get this straight," he said. "I'm to pick up the gun and aim it at you, and when I see you start your draw I can pull the trigger?"

"Yes," Preacher Jack said coldly.

Fred licked his lips a couple of times and then rubbed the sweating palms of his hands on his pants. Finally, slowly, he reached for the gun, then picked it up and pointed it toward Preacher Jack.

Preacher Jack's draw was so sudden that no one in the saloon suspected it, least of all Fred Stone. Jack's shoulder jumped and the gun was in his hand, blazing. His bullet caught Fred in the throat and Fred, surprised by the suddenness of it, dropped his gun unfired and clutched his throat. Blood spilled between his fingers as he let out a gurgling death rattle. He fell against the bar, then slid down, dead before he reached the floor.

"The ungodly have fallen into the pit they dug, and in the snare they set is their own foot caught," Preacher Jack said as he looked at the body on the floor.

"My God, did you see that?" someone asked. "Fred had the gun pointed at him and he never even got off a shot."

"That's the damnedest thing I ever saw."

"Who could beat someone that fast?" another asked.

Preacher Jack sat back down to his game. His little trick had impressed everyone in the saloon, but he knew the truth. The advantage had been his all along. Preacher Jack had learned long ago that it took more time to think about drawing than it did to draw. And if a person's mind was clouded with drink, that thinking time would be even longer. So while Fred was thinking about it, Preacher Jack was doing it.

It was an easy kill, as easy as blowing away Earl had been this morning.

Mindy figured that it had to be at least one o'clock in the morning. She had been on watch until ten, when John relieved her. She was supposed to be asleep now, but sleep wouldn't come.

The rest of the house was very quiet, and Mindy was confident that her father was sound asleep. She wished she could be as fortunate. She sighed, fluffed up her pillow, tried to find a more comfortable position, and closed her eyes.

No good. Within a moment the position was uncomfortable again, and the pillow had mysteriously grown hard. She sighed, fluffed the pillow once more, and repositioned herself. She still couldn't fall asleep.

Finally she sat up. A bar of moonlight streamed in through the window, splashed a pewter stain on the wall. Mindy got out of bed and walked over to the window, opened the curtains, and looked outside. A large cottonwood tree stood just outside the window. Its leaves moved softly in the gentle night breeze, catching the moonbeams in scattered bursts of silver. The moon was so bright that Mindy could see for miles, far across the rolling hills of the Lazy L ranch. The landscape was delineated in shades of silver and black. She felt that she had never seen anything quite so beautiful.

On impulse, she pulled a wrapper around her, then stepped out into the hall barefooted. She walked quietly through the house, then through the front door, across the porch, and out onto the ground.

The gentle breeze was still blowing, and it felt good as it moved through her hair and touched her skin. She headed directly for the bunker where she knew John stood watch.

"You're supposed to be getting some sleep," John said as she approached him. She smiled. She had known she wouldn't be able to sneak up on him.

"When did you see me?" she asked.

"I saw you the moment you stepped through the door. What are you doing out here?"

"I couldn't sleep," Mindy said, brushing the hair back from her face.

"I know," John said. "That may be part of their plan . . . just snipe at us until we get so nervous that no one can sleep. Then, when we're tired, they think they can just move in."

"It's not fear of Tucker Scarns keeping me awake, John Slocum," Mindy said in a low, throaty voice.

"Oh? What is?"

"I think you know," Mindy said. She sat down on the edge of the bunker and raised her knees. Her wrapper fell to the side and her legs glistened white in the silver splash of moonlight.

"Aren't you afraid you'll catch a chill?"

"Oh, no, I think it's lovely out here," she said. She looked directly at John. "Do you think about it?"

"About what?"

"About us . . . about what we did last night."

"I've thought about it," John admitted.

"Oh, John, it was so . . . so magnificent," Mindy said, searching for the right word. "I never knew it could be so good. Is it always so good?"

"It can be," John said. "If the man and woman are right for each other, care for each other. If it's wrong, it can be brutal for the woman."

"Oh, it could never be wrong with you," Mindy said. "It was the most wonderful night of my life."

John smiled at her and kissed her, pushing her back gently until they were both lying on the side of the bunker. His lips traveled from her mouth down along her throat, and down to the top of her nightgown. He pushed the nightgown down and kissed the flesh behind it, then moved to her breasts. He kissed each nipple, feeling her body jump with the sensations he was causing her and listening to the soft moans of pleasure which escaped from deep in her throat.

"We should have a bed with silk sheets, and a door to close," John said.

"No," Mindy said, her voice choked with passion as she spoke. "No, I want to do it here. This is perfect, absolutely perfect.

"I want you," Mindy gasped. "I want you in me."

John lowered his trousers, then moved up on her body. Mindy put her hands around behind John's butt and pulled forward, and he felt delicious sensations of total invasion.

John kissed Mindy on her neck. He could feel the muscles in her neck twitching, and he opened his mouth to suck on the creamy white skin before him. He could hear the gasps and moans of pleasure from this beautiful creature beneath him, and her hips rose wildly to meet his every thrust.

John heard Mindy's gasps and moans rise in intensity, and he could tell by the increase in her movements, and the spasmodic action of her thrusting hips, that she was nearing orgasm. He rode with her, and when they came, it was a total, all-consuming orgasm, and for an instant he felt keenly with every cell of his body that was in contact with the naked skin of Mindy.

John lay on top of Mindy for a few seconds, then rolled to one side. He put his arm out, and Mindy cuddled against it.

"I wish you had been here last year," Mindy finally said.

"Last year? Why?"

Mindy raised up on one elbow and looked down at John.

"Because then we could have done this one whole year sooner," she said.

John laughed.

"I'm serious," Mindy said.

This was the second time in as many nights that she had come to him. He wondered if he had a tiger by the tail.

9

Tucker Scarns was in the back of the general store looking over Marcus Dunne's supply of coffins. He was there to pick out a casket for Fred Stone.

"This is a nice one," Dunne offered, showing Scarns one which was polished to a soft, yellow shine. "It's one of our better models. Very popular with the women folk."

"Yeah, well, I don't guess Stone had any women folk to weep for him. I think he was from back in Mississippi or Alabama or someplace like that. No folks out here; that's why I'm takin' care of things."

"It's a Christian thing for you to do to see to his buryin'," Dunne said.

"How much is that one?" Scarns pointed to a plain, pine box.

"Oh, well, uh, that's our plainest model," Dunne said. "It is really not appropriate for displaying the body at a funeral service, or anything like that."

"I'm not going to show the son of a bitch off," Scarns explained. "I'm just buryin' him, that's all. Now how much for that one?"

"Seven dollars and fifty cents," Dunne said.

Scarns pulled out his wallet.

"Uh, plus two-fifty for preparin' the body," Dunne added quickly.

"All right," Scarns said, handing him ten dollars. "But you have to get the boy in the ground."

"Yes, sir, I'll take care of that. You can count on me. And if there are any more, uh, unfortunate events, I'll be here to take care of them as well."

Scarns started to leave, then he saw a shining black coffin, lined with red felt and trimmed with silver. He walked over and put his hand on it. The finish was smooth as silk and the gloss was such that he could see his reflection in it.

"Now that," Dunne said, perking up over Scarns's interest, "is the finest coffin we carry. It's called the 'Eternal Cloud.' It's really beautiful, don't you think?" Dunne took a cloth and polished a bit of dust away from the top.

"What you got somethin' like that here, for?" Scarns asked. "Who's gonna be buried in somethin' like that?"

Dunne cleared his throat. "Well, uh, Mr. Scarns, there is a range war going on now. And someone of importance, on one side or the other, is likely to be killed. When that happens I suspect they would like to think that there is a coffin fitting for the burial of a man of wealth and position."

"Me?" Scarns asked in quick anger. "You son of a bitch, you got that coffin for me?"

"Uh, no, sir, not exactly," Dunne said quickly, pulling his collar away from his neck. "But maybe Cap Locke would want something like this."

The frown left Scarns's face and he laughed. The genuineness of his laughter relieved Dunne of his sudden anxiety, and Dunne chuckled along with him.

"Yeah," Scarns said, running his hand over the smooth, highly polished surface again. "Yeah, I can see Cap Locke in this. It'd make a good funeral, wouldn't it?"

"Oh," Dunne gushed, "it would make a glorious funeral."

Mindy found two more opportunities to visit John in as many days. She was young, strong, and pretty, and she had a healthy interest in sex. That all combined to make her an exceptionally good lover, a skill which she eagerly developed.

It wasn't all romp with Mindy, though. There was a serious side as well as a sensuous side, and when it was time to work, Mindy worked. She proved to be a tireless laborer in the improvement of the defenses, and her skill as a markswoman had already been demonstrated.

On John's fourth day at the ranch, the alarm system he rigged was used for the first time. Lonnie was feeling good enough to take his turns on watch and he was in one of the rifle pits, about one hundred yards from the house. John and Cap were at the supper table just finishing up some roast beef Mindy had prepared, and Mindy was at the counter, washing dishes. Her Henry was leaning against the wall close by, because she was scheduled to be relieving Lonnie in about ten minutes.

The can began rattling, and for a second Cap was puzzled.

"What is that?"

"It's Lonnie!" John said, and he was the first one out of the kitchen.

Cap and Mindy were right behind him. They ran, crouching low, toward the barn. They reached the barn and paused for a moment, then Mindy started to go back to the house.

"I should go back and put out the lantern," she suggested.

"No," John said, putting out a hand to hold her back. "Leave it burning. Let them think we're still in the house, unsuspecting."

"All right," Mindy said.

John looked around the corner of the barn toward the small rise in the ground that he knew was the rifle pit where Lonnie was on watch. He searched the horizon for intruders, but saw no one.

"Mindy, you go first," John said. "Keep low, move fast. I'll keep an eye open from here. If I see anything, I'll give you cover."

Mindy didn't waste words or time. She started immediately for the rifle pit. John waited about fifteen seconds, then sent Cap after her. Another fifteen seconds and he started out on his own. He reached the pit, then squatted behind the barrier to get his breath. Mindy and Cap were still breathing hard too.

"What did you see, Lonnie?" John asked when his breathing came a little easier.

"Over there," Lonnie said, pointing off to the left.

"Do you see the little notch between those two hills?"

"Yes."

"Three or four of them are down in that draw. I saw them when they came over the top of the hill. They got careless and were outlined against the sky for a moment."

"Good job," John said.

"What do you think, John? Should we break out the Whitworth?" Cap asked.

"Not yet," John said. "I doubt that this is any more than a little foray to see what kind of firepower we have out here. If so, we don't want to show them too much, too early. It's best to let our ace stay in the hole for a while longer."

"Yeah, I guess you're right," Cap said. "What now? You have any ideas?"

"I'm going to pit number four," John said. "You go to number three. Mindy, you go to number two. Lonnie can stay here. We can fire from all four positions. That way they won't know where we are, or even how many of us there are. If they ride in much closer, we'll have them in a crossfire."

"I'm ready," Cap said.

"Me too," Mindy put in.

"All right, let's go."

Again the three defenders ran through the night, crouched low to make no silhouette which could be seen. Within a moment they were all in position. Now there was nothing to do but wait.

Silence.

The wind changed directions, and the windmill, answering the freshening breeze, swung around and began spinning. The pump piston clanked as it moved up and down, and water began splashing into the trough.

A coyote howled.

An owl hooted.

There was the scratch of hooves on the ground, the creak of riders in saddle leather.

Luke Hamrick twisted in his saddle and stared toward the house. There was a single lantern burning in the kitchen. It seemed incredible that they had managed to sneak up on them without being seen, but apparently that was just what had happened. They must be eating their supper.

"Watch where you're going," someone said, barking it in a short, angry voice.

"Shut up. You want them to hear us?" Luke warned.

"Hell, they're still in the house. They can't hear us. Not unless they got ears like dogs." That statement was followed by a short laugh.

"Luke's right," Bill Newcastle cautioned. "It's better to be safe."

"The safest thing would have been not to come out here at all," Luke said. "I think we should have waited."

"And let Preacher Jack have everything for himself?" Bill said. "You heard the way everyone's talkin' about him. Hell, it wouldn't surprise me none if Scarns didn't decide he didn't need the rest of us. He could let us go and just keep Preacher Jack."

"You know he's not gonna let Morgan, Dusty, and Shorty go," Luke said.

"Yeah, well that don't have anything to do with

us. No, the best thing we can do is take care of things ourselves, tonight. Then we can go back and get the hunnert dollars he promised us and ride on down Mexico way to spend it."

"If we're still alive to enjoy it," Luke said.

"Come on, Luke. Don't be such a yellow-belly," Bill cautioned. He raised up in his saddle and looked at the other rider. "Is everybody ready? Fire into the house. They're prob'ly in the kitchen eatin' supper. That's where the lights are. Shoot through the windows."

By now the riders were close enough for John to see shadows within shadows. It was too dark to make them out well enough for a shot, or even to determine exactly how many there were.

"Fire!" he heard one of the riders yell, and four rifles began barking.

With the muzzleflash from their rifles, John had a target. He squeezed off a round, firing just to the right and slightly below one of the muzzleflashes.

"Ow! I'm hit!"

"Goddamn!" another yelled. "Where are they?"

As soon as John fired, it was a signal for the others to open fire as well, and Cap, Mindy, and Lonnie opened up.

"What the hell? They've got an army out here!" one of the attackers shouted in a frightened voice. "Let's get the hell out of here!"

John heard the sound of hoofbeats as the nightriders turned their horses and began beating a retreat. The defenders fired three or four more times but they were just shooting in the dark with no idea as to where their targets were. It didn't really matter. The idea now was simply to run them off, and that they had done.

"All right!" John shouted. "Hold your fire, save your ammunition! They're gone!"

"Ha!" Lonnie shouted. "We won! We ran them off!"

John walked back toward the other pits, picking up first Cap, and then Mindy. Finally all four of them were gathered in pit number one where Lonnie was still excited, still flushed with victory over their successful skirmish.

"I'll bet they won't be back," Lonnie said.

"Don't count on that, Lonnie," John warned him. "They were only out here to throw a scare into us. This wasn't the full attack, not by a long shot."

"Maybe so," Lonnie said. "But if you ask me, they didn't throw the scare into us, we threw it into them."

"The boy's got a point there, John," Cap chuckled.

"Maybe so," John agreed. "But let's not get too cocky yet. We still have a ways to go before this fight's over. Mindy, I don't think they'll be back tonight, but keep as sharp a lookout as you would anyway."

"Don't worry about that," Mindy said. "A field mouse won't get by without me knowing it."

"Good," John said. "Now, the rest of us should get some sleep while we can. If they ever figure out there's only four of us, they could just wear us down."

The first pink light of dawn touched the sagebrush, and the light was soft and the air was cool. John had taken the last relief and now he sat quietly watching dawn break over the Lazy L Ranch. The last morning star made a bright pinpoint of light over the purple Cap Rock Escarpment which lay in a ragged line to the north.

He heard the kitchen door close sharply behind him and when he looked around he saw Cap walking toward the pit, carrying a coffeepot and two cups. Cap settled down beside John and poured them each a cup of coffee.

"Coffee smells mighty good," John said, taking the cup in both hands and raising it to his lips.

"Mindy's fixin' some bacon and biscuits," he said. "She'll be bringin' some out in a bit. Thought you could use this while you're waitin'."

"Good of you," John said. He blew on the coffee and sucked it noisily through his lips.

"Everything all right?" Cap asked.

"Yeah," John said. "We busted up whatever plans they had for last night."

"We're gonna whip 'em, John. Oh, I've thought all along we'd give 'em a run for their money. But I got me a gut feelin' now that we're gonna whip 'em."

John smiled. "I've put faith in your gut feelings before, Cap," he said. "I guess I can do it again." John leaned his rifle against the barrier, then got up and started out toward the open field in front of them.

"Where are you going?" Cap asked.

"I hit one of them last night," John said. "It's light enough now, thought I'd see if I could tell how bad he was hurt."

· · ·

"I'm hurt bad, Scarns. I'm gut-shot," Bill Newcastle groaned. He was lying in the bunkhouse at the Box S. "I need me a doctor."

"Ain't nothin' a doctor can do for you, Newcastle," Scarns said. "That bullet's done tore up your gizzard. You're most likely gonna die. I can have Preacher Jack say a few words."

"It . . . it weren't supposed to be like this," Hamrick said. "You said all we'd have to do is scare 'em off. We'd all get a hunnert dollars apiece, and all we had to do was scare 'em off."

"Hell, did I tell you boys to go out there last night and get yourself gut-shot?" Scarns said. "It was your idea to go out there, if you recollect."

"What gets me," Hamrick said, "is how he could see to shoot Bill in the dark like that."

"Lucky shot," Scarns suggested.

"No," Hamrick said. "No, there weren't nothin' lucky about it. Don't forget, me and Bill seen him shoot down Bagget, 'n' Bagget was the fastest gun I ever knowed."

"I was faster," Preacher Jack said quietly.

"Yeah?" Hamrick said. "Well, maybe you was and maybe you wasn't. We ain't never gonna know that, are we? But we do know Slocum was faster, 'cause we seen it. And not only that, Slocum's got eyes can see in the dark, else he couldn't of shot Bill down last night like he done."

"What are you trying to say, Hamrick?" Scarns asked. "You trying to say Slocum's not human?"

"He's human all right," Preacher Jack said. "I'll prove that soon as I run up against 'im."

"You just do that, Preacher. Right now, me 'n'

Bill want our hunnert dollars. We're gettin' out of here."

"You'll get the money when the job is done, and not before," Scarns said.

"Luke? Luke?" Newcastle cried out. He gasped a couple of times, then his last breath rattled in his throat. Preacher Jack put his hand on Newcastle's neck.

"He's dead," Preacher Jack said easily.

"You ain't gonna give me the money now?" Hamrick asked.

"I told you, you'll get it when the job's done."

Hamrick looked around the bunkhouse at Scarns, Preacher Jack, and half a dozen others who had gathered to watch Newcastle die.

"You want my opinion, this job ain't never gonna get done," Hamrick said. He started for the door. "You can keep the money, Scarns. It ain't worth dyin' for."

10

One of the things that made the Lazy L Ranch property worth owning was the water which flowed through the property. There hadn't always been a natural flow of water. The creek was little more than a seasonal bayou, a runoff from the Red River, when Cap first began ranching. Cap knew that it would be possible to connect the low spots and divert the creek, and that's just what he did.

A couple of days after the skirmish at the main house, four of Cap's lineshack riders, Brad Estes, Jimmy Peters, Mike and Matt Esterhouse, were coming back to report the tallies. The tallies were way short this year. Not only that, the four men had seen some riders pushing unbranded dogies, which they knew were some of Cap's beeves, across the property line.

As they rode back toward the big house, they saw ten or twelve beeves down at the watering hole, attended to by three riders they knew weren't from the Lazy L.

"Hey," Brad said, stopping the others. "Look down there. Anybody know those waddies?"

The other three stopped and looked down toward the watering hole.

"I ain't never seen any of 'em before," Matt said.

"By God, I have," Jimmy said. "That one fella there, the one in the red shirt, he's one of them was drivin' some of Cap's dogies yesterday."

"What are they doin' here?"

"Let's ride down and find out," Brad suggested.

"The fella in the blue shirt, he was with them too," Mike said.

"What about the other one, the one all dressed in black who's off by hisself a little? Anyone recognize him?"

"Can't say as I do," Mike said.

"He's a ugly son of bitch, ain't he?" Brad said. The others laughed nervously.

The four Lazy L riders rode down to the watering hole and stopped about fifteen yards away. The men at the watering hole watched them approach, but made no attempt to leave.

"Might I ask who you fellas are?" Matt asked.

"Folks call me Preacher Jack," the rider in black said.

"You a preacher?"

"Some say I am."

"Well, Preacher, what are you doin' here?"

"We're watering our stock," Preacher Jack said.

"You workin' for Cap Locke, are you?" Matt asked.

"Nope. Can't say as I am."

"Well, then you're waterin' the wrong stock, mister."

"What makes you say that?"

"Hell, look at 'em. They got the Lazy L brand all over their ass. Now you're either blind, or you're lyin'. Which is it?"

"You callin' us liars, mister?" the man in the red shirt said.

"Or thieves," Matt suggested.

Preacher Jack held up his hand. "It's all right, they just don't understand," he said. He looked at Matt and the others, his face as expressionless as stone. "We bought them," he said easily.

"You got a bill of sale?"

"You are a suspicious man, aren't you?"

"I want to see a bill of sale, or you ain't takin' these cows nowhere, and you're gonna get off Lazy L property," Matt said.

"Suppose I choose not to get off?" Preacher Jack asked.

"I'm ready to run you off," Matt said.

"Matt, take it easy," his brother Mike suggested.

"Take it easy, hell," Matt said. "I ain't lettin' no two-bit preacher come on land where I'm workin' and take my boss's cattle."

"You intend to stop me?" Preacher Jack asked.

"You damn right. Case you ain't noticed it, mister, we're packin' iron," Matt said. "And they's four of us to the three of you."

From the beginning there had been no expression in Preacher Jack's face, and there was nothing there now to show what he was about to do. One moment he was sitting there quietly, the next instant there was a gun in his hand. He fired twice. Matt and his brother tumbled from their saddles.

"For I am full of trouble," Preacher Jack said. "My life is at the brink of the grave."

"Jesus, Mister!" Brad said, throwing his hands up. "Who are you?"

"Cap Locke has hired a man named John Slocum. Tell him I'm looking forward to meeting him," Preacher Jack said. Preacher Jack nodded to the other two men and the three of them left, leaving the cattle behind.

Brad and Jimmy got down from their horses to look at Matt and Mike. The two brothers were dead.

"You killed two of them, did you?" Tucker Scarns said, when Preacher Jack and the others returned to the Box S Ranch.

"Yes," Preacher Jack said. He walked over to Scarns's liquor cabinet without being invited, and poured himself a drink.

"Ha!" Scarns said, hitting his fist into his open hand. He looked at the others who were standing around. "Now, that's the difference between doing it right, and making a blunder of things the way New-castle and Hamrick did. They ride out there in the middle of the night and get themselves shot up. Preacher Jack rides out in the middle of the day and shoots two of them. Word of this gets out, I reckon all the rest of Cap Locke's men will leave him. Then we'll have things our way."

"The only thing," Morgan said. "He'll still have Slocum."

"So what?" Scarns said. "Preacher Jack here can handle Slocum, right, Jack?"

"I'm looking forward to it," Preacher Jack said, pulling one of Scarns's Havana cigars from the humidor.

"That's it, John," Cap said after Brad and Jimmy rode in to report what had happened. "I'm gonna send word out to let all my men go. I'm not gonna get any more of them killed in this war. They're ranch hands, not gunmen."

"Maybe it's about time I pushed this a little," John suggested.

"What do you mean?"

"We've been sitting back, waiting for Scarns to make all the moves. Maybe we should make a move ourselves."

"What are you plannin' to do?"

"I'm going into town," John said.

"Good idea," Cap agreed. "We'll go into town and settle this once and for all."

"No," John said quickly. "I'm going into town alone."

"You can't face them all down alone."

"I don't intend to," John said. "All I plan to do is push things a little, get the ball rolling. Don't forget, we've got an ace in the hole out here. If you go in with me and we have the showdown there, we're playing their game, on their table."

"John's right, Papa," Mindy said. "We've got everything set up for them here. We can't fight them in town."

"Mr. Slocum, you'd better watch out for Preacher Jack," Brad warned. "He sent word that he was looking for you."

"Yeah, what about this here Preacher Jack fella?" Cap asked. "If you go into town, won't he be waitin' on you?"

"Preacher Jack is a little man who's used half a dozen tricks to get his reputation," John said. "I'm not concerned about Preacher Jack."

"I hope you're right," Cap said.

"Don't forget, Cap, the man we're really concerned with is Tucker Scarns. Preacher Jack is just working for him."

"Nevertheless, Preacher Jack's awful fast," Brad suggested. "He shot Matt and Mike down before their guns could even clear leather."

John smiled. "Matt and Mike were gunmen, were they?"

"Why, no, they were cowhands, that's all."

"Then don't get me wrong, Brad. I'm sure they were good men, but the fact that Preacher Jack shot them down doesn't mean anything. It was like taking candy from a baby. If you've never really seen a gun handled, you can't judge whether Preacher Jack is any good or not."

"I . . . I guess not," Brad answered.

Cap Locke went to his safe and took out some money. "Brad, Jimmy, I want you to do something for me," he said.

"Sure, Cap, anything you say," Brad answered.

Cap counted out a handful of money and gave it to him.

"This'll pay you, Jimmy, and the others off for the month. I want you to ride out and find them, give them their wages, and tell them to get lost for a while."

"Cap, you can't fire us all now. You need us," Brad said.

"I don't need any more of you gettin' yourselves killed," Cap said. "Go on, do what I say. Come on back next month. If I've won, there'll be jobs for all of you. If I've lost... Well, at least you will have gotten out without any more of you gettin' hurt."

"I can't just leave you like this," Brad said.

"Do it, Brad," Cap insisted. "I've got enough on my mind now without worrying about any more good men gettin' themselves killed in a war that don't concern them."

"Well, all right, if you say so," Brad said, taking the money reluctantly. "But I don't feel good about it."

"We'll see to it the others get their pay," Jimmy said.

"I know you will," Cap replied. "You're good men, both of you. And when this is all over, there will be a place for all of you."

"Thanks, Cap," Brad said.

"And good luck," Jimmy added.

Brad and Jimmy got back on their horses, nodded at Cap and the others, then rode off to find the few remaining hands.

"Thanks, Cap," Lonnie said.

"Thanks for what?"

"Thanks for not tryin' to pay me off like the others."

"Well, you've been through it now," Cap said. "I sorta figured you had a little more stake in it than the other fellas did."

"I do," Lonnie said. "I owe Preacher Jack for Earl, and I owe 'em for a bullet hole in my leg."

"Besides that, I figure that you bein' the foreman, you'll want to look out for your interest," Cap added.

Lonnie smiled broadly. "The foreman?" he said. "Cap, you're makin' me the foreman?"

Cap laughed. "I reckon I am," he said. "Only thing is, right now there ain't no one left for you to be foreman over. We let everyone go."

"That's all right," Lonnie said excitedly. "Soon as we settle accounts with Tucker Scarns, we'll be a ranch again. And, Cap, we'll be the best ranch in the whole state of Texas!"

Mindy followed John out to the barn, and stood beside him while he saddled his horse.

"Lonnie sure is happy," she said.

"Lonnie's a good man," John said.

"He's a boy."

"Only a couple of months younger than you. He's aged fast in the last few days."

Mindy smiled. "If I didn't know better, John Slocum, I'd say you were trying to speak for him to me."

"Maybe I am."

"Maybe I don't want anyone spoken for me. Maybe I already have the man I want."

John looked at Mindy for a long, silent moment, then put his hand on hers. "Girl, you know there can never be anything real between us," he said.

"I . . . I thought what we had was real," Mindy said.

"It was . . . and it is," John said. "As far as it goes. But, Mindy, there's a lot more to a man and a woman than what we've done."

"But it's been good," Mindy said. "You said yourself, it's been good."

"Sure, it's been good, but a man and woman can't spend all their time together in bed. There's other times too, and those times are important. Truth is, they're even more important. For times like that, you got to have someone who's settled. Someone who knows what he wants, and where he's goin'."

"Couldn't you settle here?"

"No," John said. "When this is all over, I'll be moving on."

"But . . . I thought . . ." Mindy started, then she stopped. "You didn't make me any promises," she admitted.

John took both her hands in his and looked into her face.

"You remember when I told you that it would always be good if it was right between the man and the woman?"

"Yes."

"You'll find that man, and when you do, you'll forget all about me."

"I can never forget about you, John Slocum."

John smiled. "Well, truth to tell, I don't reckon I want you to forget about me, completely. But what I mean is, you'll find a man, and it'll be right."

"And you think Lonnie is that man?"

"I can't tell you that," John said. "That's something only you can tell. But I can tell you this. I've known lots of men in my life, in war and peace, in good times and bad. I've learned to be a judge of men. It may be that judging other men is my only talent, but if it is, I'm good at it. And I'm telling you, Mindy, I've seen Lonnie from all sides now. He's a good man. A woman could do a lot worse than to settle down with someone like Lonnie."

John finished tightening the cinch, then he swung up into the saddle.

Mindy smiled sadly. "You sound like the matchmakers my mama used to tell me about."

"An honorable profession," John replied, smiling down at her.

"John, you'll come back safe?" Mindy worried.

John touched the brim of his hat. "Don't worry about that, girl," he said. "That's just what I intend to do."

11

The town didn't improve any with time. It was still the same hot, dry, fly-blown town he rode into the first time. There seemed to be a little more activity this time, though. At least, there were more horses tied to hitching rails.

John dismounted in front of the general store. He looked over to the front of the saloon and saw half a dozen horses there, all wearing Box S brands on their rumps.

The bell tinkled on the door of the general store as John stepped inside. There were three people in the store besides Dunne: a man, a woman, and a boy. The man, who didn't seem to be with the woman, was looking at boots. The woman was over on the other side, unrolling bolts of cloth to examine the fabric. The boy was eyeing a big glass bowl filled with horehound candy.

"Oh," Dunne said, when he saw John. "You'd be Mr. Slocum."

"Have we met?" John asked.

"Most assuredly, sir. I'm Marcus Dunne. Remember? The day you arrived you were kind enough to make arrangements for Mr. Bagget. I took care of him for you."

"Yes, I remember," John said. He saw the woman looking at him, and he tipped his hat. She made a point of turning away, but before she did, John saw the look in her eyes, the little lights which glowed way in the bottom that said she was curious. If she had the opportunity and no one would ever find out, she would satisfy that curiosity. "Go ahead and take care of the lady," John invited.

"Yes, of course," Dunne said, clearing his throat nervously. "It won't take too long, then I'll be right with you."

"Good," John said. He looked at the boy and saw himself when he was a youngster back in Georgia. He remembered leaving the farm and going into town with his father. There was always a piece of horehound candy in it for John and his brother. John reached into the bowl and took a piece of the golden-brown candy, then handed it to the boy.

"Gee, thanks," the boy said, popping it into his mouth.

"It was always my favorite too," John said, smiling.

"Really? You're not just foolin' me?" the boy asked.

"I'm not just fooling," John answered.

"I know you," the boy said easily. "You're the fella shot Bagget. I seen you do it, right through this window."

The smile left John's face. The bittersweet memory of his youth passed. He was no longer a Georgia farm boy, he was a drifter. The hands that were molded to fit the plow now fit the handle of a Colt .44.

"I reckon you got me pegged, boy," John said simply.

"Timothy," the boy's mother said sharply, "come over here."

"He's the one, Mama," Timothy insisted. "I seen him. He's terrible fast with a gun."

"Come over here at once!" the woman said, and the curious lights in her eyes were tinged with fear— not terror, but just enough fear to add excitement to the situation. John saw tiny perspiration beads break out above her upper lip, and her cheeks flushed a becoming crimson.

"I'm going to be just as fast as he is when I grow up," Timothy said.

"You stay over here with me, and don't bother Mr. Slocum," the woman said.

John turned away from the boy. Incidents like this made him feel uncomfortable. He didn't want to be a hero to the boy for the wrong reason. And he didn't want to be the subject of this woman's sexual fancy, but he seemed to be both. It wasn't a new experience for him and it was too late to change things now. The best thing to do was just avoid the situation whenever he could.

"We'll be back later, Mr. Dunne," the woman said, shoving the bolt of cloth back onto the table.

"Come, Timothy, we must go."

"Mama, I want to stay. He might shoot another man."

"Timothy!" the woman gasped. She grabbed her son by the hand and pulled him toward the front door.

"Oh, you needn't hurry off, Mrs. Abernathy," Dunne called to her. "I have two nice bolts of blue cotton in the back you haven't seen yet."

"We'll be back," Mrs. Abernathy called over her shoulder, and the bell on the door rang again as she pushed through it, dragging Timothy outside with her.

"Wait on the gentleman, Mr. Dunne," the man at the boot shelf said. "I'll look around some more."

Mr. Dunne rubbed the few thin strands of pale hair which lay across his shining head and walked over to stand in front of John.

"Mrs. Abernathy is a nice lady," he said. "She was very pretty once, but her husband was thrown from a horse a couple of years ago and she's been having to make dresses for a livin'. She's good at it, but the work's hard and it's beginnin' to tell."

"I think she's still a pretty woman," John said.

Dunne smiled nervously. "Yes, she is, she is," he said. "Didn't mean to say she wasn't." He lowered his voice. "If you're interested, her husband can't take care of her in any way, if you know what I mean. I've never heard tell of her doin' anything, but you know she's got to be wantin' a man ever now 'n' again."

"You've got a mean mouth, mister," John said, glaring at the clerk.

Dunne cleared his throat and put his finger to his

collar to pull it away from his neck. "Didn't mean nothin' by that," he mumbled quickly. "Just makin' an observation, that's all."

"I'm not interested in your observation," Slocum said.

"No, sir, of course not. What can I do for you, now?"

"This is for the boy's candy," John said, handing Dunne a penny.

"Mighty generous of you. All the children like horehound. That's why I keep a goodly supply at all times." Dunne took the penny and put it in the cash register.

"I'll be needing some medical supplies," John said.

"Medical supplies?"

"Yes, bandages, liniment, a little laudanum if you have it."

"Oh, my. If you don't mind my askin', why do you need all that stuff, Mr. Slocum?"

"There's been an accident," John said.

"Where?"

"Out at the Lazy L. It's Cap Locke," John explained.

"Heavens! What happened?"

"He was thrown off a horse this morning," John said. The man at the boot shelf looked around in interest. That was just what John wanted him to do.

"Must be pretty bad if you have a need for all this stuff," Dunne said as he began filling the order.

"Bad enough," John said.

"I'm afraid we ain't got a doc in Sixgun," Dunne went on. "Though I think there might be one down to Turkey."

"I won't be needin' a doc," John said. "I know some doctoring, so I reckon I'll be tending to him myself."

"Anyone lookin' after him now, while you're in town?"

John shook his head. "No one left," he said. "All his men deserted him."

Dunne's eyebrows raised in surprise. "All of them, you say? You mean Cap Locke's out there all alone?"

"That's what I mean, mister," John said.

"Oh, my, this . . . this certainly is news," Dunne said.

John heard the bell tinkling on the front door. When he glanced around he saw that the man at the boot shelf was gone, hurrying across the street toward the saloon. John smiled. The man would no doubt be converting that information into a free drink in about half a minute.

"What do I owe you?" John asked.

"Let's see," Dunne said. He started figuring on a small pad, stopping once to sharpen the pencil with his teeth. "That comes to . . . three dollars and twenty cents."

The clerk began putting the supplies in a little cloth bag. Then he slid them across the counter.

"Oh, Mr. Slocum," Dunne ventured. "Is there any chance that Cap Locke might die?"

"There's probably a very good chance," John replied.

"If he does," Dunne said, "I think you ought to know that in addition to the normal coffins that I carry, I have an exceptionally fine model known as the 'Eternal Cloud.' I'd be mighty privileged to let you view it if you're interested."

"No, thanks," John answered.

"Well, I just thought I'd let you know," Dunne added weakly.

John glared at him again, then took the stuff he had bought outside and began packing it in his saddlebags. He was aware that by now several sets of eyes were watching him from various locations in the town. When the stuff was packed, he walked across the street to the saloon, pushed the batwing doors open, and stepped inside. The barkeep, Tom Maloney, greeted him warmly. Except for the people at the Lazy L, Tom Maloney was the only friendly person John had encountered since arriving in this town.

"Howdy, Mr. Slocum," Maloney said. Without being asked, he poured a glass of Old Overholt and slid it toward John. John paid him, then took a drink. It was good whiskey, not the stuff colored with rusty nails and flavored with tobacco juice a person often found in such out-of-the-way saloons, and which was served in this saloon to less preferred customers.

"Thanks," John said.

A tall, bearded man was standing at the opposite end of the bar. He tossed his drink down, then turned and looked at John.

"I hear a rumor that Cap Locke is bad hurt," he said.

"It's not a rumor," John answered easily.

"Folks is sayin' he won't live till dawn," Maloney said. "Is that true?"

John nodded solemnly. "I'm afraid it is," he said.

"Cap Locke is a good man," Maloney said.

"He's dyin', is he?" the man at the end of the bar said. He chuckled. "Well now, ain't that just too bad?"

John looked at the man with narrowed eyes. He'd never seen this person before, but it was obvious the man was pushing.

"Who are you?" John asked.

"The name's Fergus Gant."

"The name doesn't mean anything," John said.

"I'm a rider for Tucker Scarns. You can understand that I'm all tore up Locke is hurt so bad," Gant said sarcastically. He laughed. "Yeah, I'm just awful upset about it."

"If he's hurt bad enough, he might need a preacher," Maloney suggested in a quiet, cryptic voice.

"What?" John asked.

"If he does, I know where one is," Maloney went on.

John looked at Maloney and saw the barkeep's eyes cut slightly toward the back of the saloon. He was trying to tell John something.

John glanced in the mirror behind the bar and saw two men sitting at a table in the back. The two men were studying their drinks very closely. One of them was wearing a red shirt. The other was dressed all in black. John knew this was Preacher Jack.

So, this was what Maloney was saying. Gant was making the play, but he wasn't the main one. He was just fronting for Preacher Jack. The plan was that when the ball opened, John would be concentrating on Gant while Preacher Jack would have a free shot at him. It was a pretty smooth plan and it might have worked had the barkeep not called John's attention to Preacher Jack.

"Thanks," John answered. "I see what you mean."

"What about Mindy?" Maloney asked. "How's she taking it?"

"I'm afraid the girl's taking it pretty hard," John went on. "She's out there now, packing to leave soon as Cap cashes in."

"You might as well ride out of here too, Slocum," Gant taunted, continuing his job of needling. "You ain't got a job, you ain't got a friend. You ain't got nothin' to keep you here. You'd best just get on out of here."

John took another swallow of his drink.

"Don't see as I need to be in that big a hurry," he said easily. Now that he knew what was in store for him he felt very relaxed. The fact that they didn't know he knew gave him a slight advantage. Not much of one, when he considered that it would be his one gun to their three, but it was enough.

John knew that Preacher Jack never went into any fight unless he figured the odds to be decidedly on his side. This time he had miscalculated. He hadn't counted on the barkeep tipping John off as to the play.

"You seem awfully anxious for me to leave," John said to the man who was taunting him. "But I think I'll stay."

"Why? There ain't gonna be nothin' left for you."

"That's not quite true," John said. "You see, Cap told me I could have his stock and his ranch after he dies. That's going to be pretty quick. If this medicine don't work fast, I've got me a pretty good spread."

Gant glanced at the two men at the table. It wasn't really a glance, just a flicker of the eyes, but John knew that they were about to make their move, and he was ready for them.

"You ain't gonna live long enough to doctor that fool," Gant said.

The two men at the table suddenly stood and whirled around, guns in their hands and blazing.

Bullets crashed into the bar beside John, and glass exploded on the shelves behind. John had already started for his own gun when he saw them make their move. It was in his hand as fast as the guns were in the hands of his two would-be murderers, and John's aim was more true. John fired twice, the shots coming so close together that they sounded like one sustained explosion.

The gunman in the red shirt caught a ball right between his eyes. He pitched back, dead before he hit the floor. Preacher Jack was hit high in the chest. He dropped his gun and slapped his hand over the wound, then looked down in surprise as blood squirted through his fingers, turning his black jacket bright red. He staggered toward the bar, then slid down to a sitting position.

"How'd you do that?" he gasped in surprise.

John turned his pistol toward Gant, but Gant, who was only fronting for Preacher Jack, had already thrown his gun away and was standing there with his hands up.

"I give it up, Slocum! Don't shoot me! For God's sake, don't shoot me!"

John saw Preacher Jack's lips moving, and he moved closer so he could hear.

"You understand why I did it this way, don't you, Slocum? I was afraid you might be faster'n me. I wanted to give myself a little edge." He tried to laugh, but it came out more of a gasp. "I always thought to give myself a little edge. The verses from Psalms, those were to give me a little edge."

"You're dying, Preacher Jack," John said. "You got a verse from Psalms for this?"

Preacher Jack smiled, then coughed, and flecks of blood came from his mouth. "Evil shall slay the wicked, and those who hate the righteous will be punished," he said. He breathed hard a couple of times. Then his head fell to one side and his eyes clouded over with death.

"Amen," John added. Slocum looked over at the gunman in the red shirt. He lay flat on his back, a pool of blood on the floor beside him.

"You killed 'em both deader than hell," one of the other patrons said.

John looked back toward the bar and saw the two bullet marks near where he had been standing. One of the slugs had dug a hole in the side of the bar, missing him by less than an inch. The second bullet had skidded across the top, leaving a deep furrow, then smashing into a shelf of whiskey bottles behind the bar. Maloney was standing nearby, holding his arm. Blood was running down his forearm, dripping through his fingers.

"Were you hit, Maloney?" John asked in surprise.

"No," Maloney answered. "Just a splinter of glass, that's all."

"I'm sorry about all this," John said. He looked at Gant. "I'm even sorrier I didn't make it a clean sweep."

"I didn't have no choice, Mr. Slocum," Gant pleaded. "Preacher Jack, he made me do this! He said he'd kill you, and I wouldn't be in no danger!"

"Put not your trust in false prophets, for surely they shall lead you astray," John said.

"Yes, sir, yes, sir," Gant said, shaking his head. "I know that now, Mr. Slocum. Truly, I know that now."

John sighed. "I want you to take a message back to Scarns," he said.

"I will, I will," Gant said. "You just tell me what you want me to say and, so help me God, I'll say it."

"Tell Scarns there's no one left out there but me," John said. "Tell him if he wants me, he's going to have to come and get me."

"You want me to tell him that?" Gant asked in surprise.

"Tell him," John insisted.

"You got it. I'll tell him," Gant said, starting toward the door. "You can count on it . . . I'll tell him." He ran across the boardwalk and a moment later John heard rapid hoofbeats as Gant rode out of town at a gallop.

Shortly after Gant left, the doors swung open and Dunne hurried in. He saw the two bodies lying on the floor and he clucked his tongue and shook his head.

"My, my," he said. "What happened here?"

"Slocum killed Preacher Jack and Percy Deekus," one of the patrons said.

"You'll have to get someone else to make arrangements for them, Dunne," John said. "I've got my own to worry about."

"Yes, I understand," Dunne said. "I'm sure Mr. Scarns will be willing to see to it." He looked at the patrons. "There's free drinks for anyone who'll help me get these gents over to the back of my store."

Four men got up and, with two on each body, the dead men were carried out. Dunne left behind them, giving them instructions on where to go.

"Mr. Slocum, I don't know how smart it was for you to tell all that to Gant," Maloney said. He had just finished tying a bandage around his cut arm.

"Why not?" Slocum asked.

"Scarns himself will be comin' out to the Lazy L, now, just as sure as a gun's iron."

"Good," John said. He smiled. "That's exactly what I want him to do."

12

The wagon had already seen quite a few years of duty and over that time the sun had bleached the wooden body white. When it got hot, as it was now, it also gave off a pungent smell.

Tucker Scarns was sitting on the back of the wagon when Fergus Gant came riding in, his horse lathered with the exertion of the run. Scarns, who was a big man with a walrus moustache, got down from the wagon and glared at Gant. He didn't like to see a horse mistreated that way, especially if the horse belonged to him.

"Here," he growled. "What's the reason for treatin' that animal like that?"

"Mr. Scarns," Gant said. "I just had a run-in with John Slocum."

Scarns smoothed his moustache and narrowed his blue eyes.

"Did you now?" he said. "And he's the one set you to runnin' like that?"

"Yes. No."

A handful of Scarns's men, seeing Gant ride in at a gallop, had drifted over to listen to the conversation.

"Well, which is it, Gant? Yes or no?" one of them asked.

"He didn't run me out, if that's what you're gettin' at," Gant said, trying to defend his action. "But he did send a message to you, Mr. Scarns."

"Oh, he did, did he? And what is the message?"

"Cap Locke is bad hurt," Gant said. "He was throwed from a horse. Word is, he'll be dead by tomorrow mornin'."

Scarns grinned broadly. "Well, now, you don't say!" He looked around at the others. "Men, it looks like the Bar S just grew another ranch."

"No," Gant put in quickly.

Scarns looked at Gant in surprise. "No? What do you mean, no? Is Locke gonna die or ain't he?"

"Yes," Gant said. "But Slocum says he's takin' over the ranch. He says he's takin' it over and if you want it, you're gonna have to come and get it."

"Is that a fact?" Scarns said. "What about Cap Locke's men? Are they sidin' in with Slocum?"

"No, they ain't," Gant said. "They all done left. They deserted the ranch soon as Locke got hurt. Near as I can figure it, Slocum is gonna be out there all by hisself."

Scarns smiled broadly and slapped the side of the wagon.

"By God! I've got it now!" he said.

"I'm not so sure about that," Gant suggested cautiously.

Scarns looked at Gant. "What do you mean?"

"This here Slocum," Gant said, "he's not like anyone you've ever run across before."

"Now you're soundin' like Luke Hamrick when he come back spoutin' off as to how this Slocum had eyes could see in the dark, how he was so much faster'n Bagget."

"Luke was right," Gant said. "I'm tellin' you, Mr. Scarns, John Slocum ain't no ordinary man."

"Of course he's an ordinary man," Scarns insisted. "Hell, he's human, ain't he? He ain't no ghost, is he?"

"Oh, I'm not sayin' he's a ghost or anythin' like that. It's just that he's the fastest man with a gun I ever seen."

"You seen Preacher Jack shoot Fred Stone when Stone already had a gun in his hand, didn't you?" Morgan asked.

"Yeah, I seen that," Gant agreed.

"Are you tellin' me that this here Slocum is faster'n that?"

"I reckon that's just what I am tellin' you," Gant said.

"You wanna tell Preacher Jack that?" Morgan asked, and the others laughed at the suggestion.

"Don't reckon I can tell him that," Gant said.

Morgan laughed. "Figured you'd be too yellow to tell Preacher Jack you seen someone faster'n he is."

"Yellow ain't got nothin' to do with it," Gant said. "I can't tell 'im, 'cause Slocum just killed Preacher Jack. Percy Deekus too. Killed 'em both at the same time."

"Was it a fair fight?" Scarns asked.

"No, it wasn't no fair fight at all," Gant said.

"Didn't figure it would be," Morgan said.

Scarns smiled. "I don't know what you're so worried about if it wasn't no fair fight. If Slocum killed them that way, that don't prove nothin'. It wouldn't be no trick to kill Preacher Jack if you drygulched him."

"It wasn't Slocum who done the drygulchin'," Gant said. "It was Preacher Jack and Percy."

"What are you talkin' about?" Morgan asked.

"I'm sayin' they laid for him, and they had their guns out first, but he still killed them."

"Maybe you better tell me what happened," Scarns suggested.

"Preacher Jack got this idea," Gant said. "I was to call Slocum down, get him to brace me. Preacher Jack and Percy would be off to one side, like as if they wasn't payin' no attention to what was goin' on, you see. Then, when Slocum braced me, they was gonna kill him before he even knowed they was there. It would look like they was just backin' my play, but the plan was for them to just drygulch him, right out. Only thing is, it didn't work out like that. They drawed on him when he wasn't even lookin', but," Gant paused to get his breath, "I thought Bagget was fast and I thought Preacher Jack was fast. Truth to tell, I've seen some fast guns in my day. But I'm not lyin' when I tell you that Slocum is quick as thought. He had his gun out and blazin' before you could blink an eye. And he put two shots together so fast it sounded like one. Not only that, but Percy and Preacher Jack was standin' apart so as not to make an easy target, but that didn't make no never mind to

Slocum. No sir, he got Percy between the eyes and Preacher Jack in the heart."

"And what about you?" Morgan Cole asked. "What was you doin' all this time?"

"Yeah," Dusty wanted to know. "You was supposed to be with them. How come you wasn't killed too?"

"I hadn't even started my draw till it was all over," Gant explained. "I don't mind tellin' you, I thought I'd cashed in my chips... figured I'd be eatin' my supper in hell. Anyway, I never said I was good with a gun, and Preacher Jack told me I wouldn't have to be. He told me he and Percy would take care of Slocum for me. But the next thing you know they was both lyin' dead on the floor and Slocum had his gun pointin' right at me."

"But he didn't kill you?" Scarns asked.

"No."

"Why not?"

"I don't know. I reckon he knew he could kill me any time he wanted. And I reckon he wanted to make sure I got the message to you. It's crazy, Mr. Scarns. It's like he's wantin' you to come out after him, even with him bein' all alone and all."

"Who the hell is this Slocum, anyway?" Scarns asked.

"Scarns, I've heard tell of him before," Morgan offered. "Friend of mine was up in Cheyenne a year or so back. He told me he seen Slocum in action up there."

"Seems to me he did some pretty good shootin' in Dodge City oncet, too," Dusty added.

"They say he's better'n Hickock and Earp put together."

"Shut up, all of you. You sound like a bunch of scared women," Scarns said. He rubbed his chin. "Let me think about this for a moment."

"You can think all you want," Morgan said. "But the truth is, I don't think you're gonna get anyone to face him down. I'm pretty good with a gun but I wouldn't want to go up against him, not if I had two more just as good as me at my side."

"I don't intend to face him down," Scarns said. "I'm no fool. There's other ways of takin' care of him."

"How?"

"Didn't you hear Gant say that he's out at the Lazy L all alone?"

"Yeah, waitin' for you to come get him," Morgan said.

Scarns chuckled. "Yeah, well, I'm goin' to go get him, all right. But not the way he thinks."

"What you got in mind?"

"We're all goin' after him," Scarns said. "It don't matter how fast a man is, he can't face down a whole army. Tomorrow mornin', come first light, we're goin' to be ridin' onto the Lazy L. All of us. We'll be goin' in like an army, twenty men, every one of us armed with repeatin' rifles. By God, I'd like to see him stop that."

"I don't know," Gant said. "You don't know Slocum. You ain't seen him close up like I have."

"Goddamn, Gant, you that big a coward?" Morgan asked. "I don't mind tellin' you that I won't go up against him alone. But with twenty men, ridin' in like an army against one man? Shit, they ain't a man ever lived I wouldn't face that way, be it Hickock, Earp, Billy the Kid, or John Slocum. And if you ain't man enough to ride with us with that kind of odds in our favor, then you ain't no man at all."

"Thanks, Morgan," Scarns said. Scarns looked at Gant. "What do you say?" he asked.

Gant rubbed his fingers through his hair. "I don't know," he said.

"You can always ride off like Hamrick done," Morgan went on. "The rest of us will just divide up your money."

"No," Gant said. "No, I've stuck it out this far, I'll go the rest of the way with you."

"All right," Scarns said. He smiled broadly, then climbed up on the wagon. "Men, I want you to get your rifles and pistols ready. Go into town and have a couple of drinks tonight if you want. I'll tell Maloney that the liquor's on me. About three in the mornin', we're gonna be pullin' out. Before sunrise we'll be on the Lazy L. Come first light, we hit Slocum. He'll breakfast in hell . . . we'll eat in the Lazy L kitchen!"

Scarns shouted the last line, and the men let out a cheer, then broke up to go back to the bunkhouse and prepare their weapons. This was what they had signed on for, what they had been waiting for. The fact that the fight was going to be twenty to one made it great sport for them. The fact that it was Slocum made it even better. From now on they would all be able to claim a part in the killing of John Slocum. Next time any man's gun was put out for hire it would be worth a little more.

Tucker Scarns poured himself a glass of whiskey, then held it out and looked at it. The amber fluid caught a beam of sunlight and glowed bright, as if it were lit by some internal flame. Scarns squinted his eyes as he looked at the fire in the whiskey, and he recalled another fire at another place, just two years ago.

He was riding for Jesse Chisholm then. Chisholm had just bought out a man named Art Conners, a neighboring rancher, paying him top dollar for his cattle and land. Scarns heard Conners was leaving Texas, giving up ranching to return to Virginia where he planned to use the money he got from Chisholm to buy a farm and raise tobacco.

On the night before Conners was to leave, Scarns rode over to see him. Recognizing him as one of Chisholm's men, Conners let him in. They talked, Scarns said Chisholm had offered to let Scarns ride along to help protect the money. Conners laughed and patted his money belt, said the money was perfectly safe as long as it was there.

When Conners turned his back on Scarns a moment later, Scarns hit him over the head with the butt of his gun. Conners went out like a light. Scarns took the money, then smashed the lantern against the floor, setting the house afire.

Scarns figured only to set the fire to cover his escape. He thought Conners would wake up in time to get out. Conners didn't wake up, though, and neither did his family. Conners, his wife, and their two children were killed in the blaze.

When people in the county discovered it the next day they found an open whiskey bottle by Conners's body. The inquest determined that Conners had been celebrating the sale, that he had come downstairs after the rest of the family was in bed to have a few drinks. He must have gotten drunk and either passed out, or fallen and knocked himself out, knocking over the lantern.

The Conners family had the biggest funeral ever held in the county, and Tucker Scarns was one of the pallbearers. He waited for three months to make sure all suspicion had passed, then he left. He used the money he stole from Conners to buy beef to stock the Box S Ranch.

No one knew his story. No one ever even suspected that Conners had been robbed. They figured the money had burned up in the fire. Sometimes the thought of what he had done bothered Scarns a little . . . just a little.

When he did think about it, it gave him all the more reason why he needed to succeed in building the biggest ranch in Texas. After going this far he didn't intend to be stopped now. He wouldn't be stopped by Cap Locke, and he wouldn't be stopped by John Slocum.

Tomorrow the Lazy L and its water would belong to him.

Tucker Scarns raised the glass to his lips and the fire in the fluid winked out. He tossed the whiskey down to blot out the thoughts. It didn't pay to think too much before you killed a man.

13

The setting sun, losing both heat and brilliance, seemed poised in the west above the High Plains. A dark gray haze was beginning to gather in the notches of Cap Rock Escarpment, hanging there like drifting smoke. The red sandy loam was dotted with blue cedar and mesquite, limned in gold from the setting sun.

Onto this scene rode Mindy Locke, picking her way along the familiar rim line to look out over the sweeping grandeur of the Palo Duro Canyon that was her home. She picked her way carefully along a trail that led to a private place, a secret glen she had discovered and to which she often came when troubled or when she wanted to be alone, just to think.

The trail climbed up the backside of a bluff,

through a cathedral arch of cedar trees, across a level bench of soft grass and fluttering yellow, red, and blue wildflowers, to a rocky precipice on the edge of the rim. It was the precipice which made the ride worthwhile, for from it Mindy could see the entire canyon floor and the ranch, including the main house, the barn, and the bunkhouse where the hands slept when they weren't out on the range or in one of the lineshacks.

From here, too, she could see the approach to the canyon, south all the way to Quitaque Creek, and north across Little Red River which watered the Lazy L, all the way to Prairie Dog Town Fork. From here she would be able to see John as he returned from Sixgun.

As Mindy thought of John, she felt a sweet aching in her loins and she recalled the many times they had made love. She had convinced herself that she was in love with John and when this was all over and he left, she would leave with him, going where he went, making his home her home.

When she suggested that to John, though, he had turned her down. He had been very subtle and sensitive to her feelings, but he had told her in so many words that he wouldn't appreciate her going with him. He had even suggested that Lonnie might be a more appropriate partner for her.

Mindy had been hurt at first, but she had been thinking about it ever since. And the more she thought about it, the more she began to believe that perhaps John was right.

Maybe not about Lonnie. That was something that would happen if it was meant to happen. But Slocum was right that she shouldn't leave this ranch to throw herself at him.

She did love him, but she loved him for what he had done and what he was doing for her father. She also loved him for what he had done for her.

It was easy to see what he had done for her father. For his old friend Cap Locke, Slocum had put himself in a fight that wasn't his. He had faced and would face the guns of determined and desperate men to help save the ranch.

For her it was a little more subtle to pinpoint what he had done. But though it was subtle, it was very, very real. He had awakened in Mindy an awareness of sexual pleasure. He had shown her the joys she could experience by being a woman.

Mindy loved him, there was no question about that. But she no longer felt she had to love him to make right the things they had done together. The moments of intimacy they had shared were both satisfying and fulfilling, and needed no other justification.

Mindy had wanted to become a woman, and thanks to John, she had. Now that she understood that, the love she felt for him was more mature. It was forgiving and less desperate. It was also less demanding, and that meant it was time for her to get on with her life. She would stay here and watch this ranch grow to the dream that she shared with her father.

On the ranch below, a wispy pall of wood smoke lay its diaphanous haze over the house and Mindy knew that her father was preparing supper. Cooking was a task they shared equally since the cook left, especially as Mindy often had to be on guard, as she was now. For, though Mindy was using this quiet time for thought, she had actually come up here to stand watch.

About three-quarters of the way back to the ranch Slocum stopped, then got down out of the saddle to let his horse take a blow. John lit a quirly and stood there beside his mount, smelling the warm sunlight on the Morgan's flesh. The horse began to crop at the short buffalo grass.

John watched the sun's golden fireball slip down over the horizon, spreading the sky with crimson, belly-lighting the clouds with purple. This was home for John . . . not Cap's ranch, not some hotel in a town or city, not even a particular state or section of the country. Home was being on the trail alone, having just said goodbye somewhere and with no particular place to go.

"Horse," he said aloud, "wouldn't it be good if we could just head due west now?"

The horse whickered, and John chuckled.

"No, I'm not going to leave Cap until this business is all settled. Don't worry about that. But a fellow does get a little homesick every now and again, even if he doesn't really have a home."

John thought about the events in Sixgun. He had intended to push the issue, forcing Scarns to make his move. He was certain now that he had done just that. What he hadn't planned was his run-in with Preacher Jack. That had been an unexpected bonus.

John had run across a dozen Preacher Jacks in his lifetime. Men like Preacher Jack built cheap reputations, then depended on the fear they caused to provide them with their edge. They had probably been bullies when they were children, and they continued to be bullies after they grew up. The only difference was their childish games were much more deadly, once they were full grown.

Tucker Scarns was much more dangerous. Scarns would have his killing done for him as long as he could find someone to do it. That left Scarns safe to cause as much misery as he could. Men like Scarns came out only when they knew they had all the odds on their side.

With the defenses he, Cap, Mindy, and Lonnie had built at the Lazy L, the odds weren't overwhelmingly in Scarns's favor. But by making him think that John was the only one left, Scarns would think they were.

Just as he had used Preacher Jack's weakness against him, John hoped to play the same trick against Tucker Scarns. Slocum was fast with a gun; there was no denying that. But he had survived all these years on the hard trail by his wits as much as he had by the speed of his hand.

John gave his horse a few more minutes' rest, then ground out the butt of his quirly. He climbed into the well-worn saddle and started up again. He was hungry and he realized that he hadn't eaten anything since breakfast. He hoped they would hold supper for him.

Mindy saw John approaching from the south, so she rode back down the canyon rim to meet him. She knew John had had some sort of plan in mind when he rode into town. She wanted to see if his plan had worked.

"Hello," John said, smiling as Mindy rode out to meet him.

"Hello, yourself," Mindy replied. "How did it go in town?"

"I had a run-in with a few of Scarns's men," John said. "But I got the message across." John saw movement in the barn and his eyes narrowed. Mindy smiled.

"It's the line riders," she said. "They decided on their own not to ride away."

"Do they know there's a big fight coming tomorrow?"

"Tomorrow?" Mindy asked.

"Unless I miss my guess, Scarns will be attacking us first thing in the morning," John said.

"Oh," Mindy replied softly.

John reached over and patted Mindy's hand.

"Don't worry," he said. "We'll be ready for him."

"I know we will," she answered. "But I can't help but be a little frightened."

"Good," John said.

"Good? You think it's good that I'm frightened?"

"Yeah, sure. In the first place, it tells me that you understand this isn't going to be some game. And in the second place, it reassures me that you'll be careful."

"I'll be careful, all right," Mindy said, smiling.

"What do I smell?" John asked.

"I don't know. Pa fixed supper tonight."

"Whatever it is, he did it up right," John said.

Cap Locke had cooked steaks over a mesquite fire. He fried potatoes, then scrambled eggs in them, and topped it off with fresh biscuits.

Lonnie sat down with Slocum and Mindy.

"Am I right?" Cap Locke asked as he served up the meal. "Is tomorrow gonna be a big day for us?"

"It looks that way," John said.

"That's exactly what I thought. That's why I figured we'd eat good tonight." He served himself a large helping of potatoes and eggs. "What happened? How can you be sure he'll be in tomorrow?"

John chuckled. "I sent word that you'd been in a bad accident, would probably cash in your chips by morning. I told them Mindy was packing to leave and all your hands were already gone. I said you'd left the ranch to me, and if Scarns wanted it he was going to have to come and take it away from me. I let it out that it would be easy for him because I'd be the only one here."

"I reckon Scarns is gonna have quite a little surprise when he does come in," Cap said. "'Cause you ain't gonna be the only one here. Not by a long shot."

"I see the line riders stayed," John said.

Cap smiled proudly. "I offered them the chance to leave, but they wouldn't take it. They're anxious to be useful."

"I'm glad for their loyalty," John said as he cut a piece of steak, then transferred it to his mouth. "But, to be honest, I'd just as soon keep them out of the way for a while, hold them in reserve in case we need them."

"They won't like that too much," Cap suggested. "They've got their fightin' dander up now."

"I'm sure they have. But the way we've got it planned, the crossfire, the dynamite charges and the Whitworth, we can handle it best alone."

"What do you mean, alone?" Lonnie asked anxiously.

"I mean just the four of us. You, me, Cap, and Mindy."

Lonnie smiled broadly. "Thanks," he said. "For a minute there, I thought you might be includin' me with the line riders."

"You've been a part of this fight from the beginning, Lonnie," John said. "I see no reason to leave you out now."

"Especially since you're the foreman," Mindy added, smiling at him.

"Yeah," Lonnie said proudly. "Yeah, I guess I am at that, aren't I?"

"You think Scarns will come in himself tomorrow?" Cap asked. "Or will he just send Preacher Jack?"

"We don't have to worry about Preacher Jack any more," John said as he buttered a biscuit.

"Why not?" Lonnie asked. "I owe that son of a bitch for Earl. Excuse the language, Mindy."

"Hope you're not upset, Lonnie," John said, "but I had to take care of that little debt for you."

"What do you mean?" Cap asked.

"Preacher Jack drew on me," John said. "I had to kill him."

"You mean he's already dead?" Lonnie asked.

"Yeah."

"You're not mad, are you, Lonnie?" Mindy asked.

Lonnie smiled sheepishly. "No," he said. "I wasn't goin' to back off from him, but I don't mind tellin' you, I wasn't lookin' forward to seein' him again, either. I hope you don't think the less of me for that."

"Think the less of you?" Mindy said, looking at him in a new light. "A boy would have blustered and bragged as to how he wanted Preacher Jack all to himself. A man would act just the way you have." Mindy put her hand on Lonnie's arm. "It's comforting to know I'll have a man in the pit next to mine, and not a boy."

Lonnie cleared his throat, then smiled at Cap and John.

"You'd better watch that girl's eyes, Lonnie," Cap chuckled. "That's the same look Earline got about the time she caught me." Cap looked over at John. "You recollect that look, John?"

"Earline never looked at me like that," John said. "You were the only one she had eyes for."

"I guess I was the lucky one, at that," Cap said.

"I'd never fault her for it," John went on. "She chose a good man." He looked pointedly at Mindy. "Looks like Mindy's about to do the same."

Lonnie smiled broadly and Mindy looked at John, thanking him with her eyes.

"How many you reckon will be comin' in tomorrow?" Cap asked.

"My guess is Scarns will bring in every man he's got. There'll be plenty enough to go around. I'd say fifteen to twenty, at least," John answered.

"Say twenty," Cap said. "That'll just be five apiece." He laughed.

"What is it, Papa?" Mindy asked. "What are you laughing at?"

"I mind the time durin' the War, we was fightin' at Henderson's Gap. The colonel says to us, he says, 'Boys, the Yankees got us outnumbered five to one. Five to one. That means ever' one's got to do their part.' Well sir," Cap went on, "the fightin' commenced, and after a while the colonel seen one of our men leanin' up ag'in a tree just suckin' on a straw like as if he was out there fishin' or passin' the time of day. 'Cooter?' the colonel calls. 'Cooter, didn't you hear me tell that we was outnumbered five to one?' 'Yes, sir,' Cooter says. Then he took that straw outa his mouth and studied the end of it real casual and he says to the colonel, 'But colonel, I done got my five.'"

Everyone around the table broke up in laughter at Cap's joke. It was just the thing to break the tension. Finally, Slocum stood up and looked at the others. "Cap, I'm glad you fixed us a good meal, because we probably won't get a good sleep. We're going to spend the night outside, taking turns on watch."

"I don't feel like going to sleep, anyway," Mindy said.

"You better try, Mindy," Lonnie suggested. He was already beginning to act protective toward her.

"What about the Whitworth? Is it ready to go?" John asked.

"She's all laid in with powder and shell standing by," Cap said excitedly.

"Good. They likely don't know what kind of firepower they'll face. When they come tomorrow, we're going to hit them with everything we got."

Lonnie chuckled again. "I'm gonna get my five," he promised.

14

"I'll be needing a place where I can see everything," John said.

Cap chuckled. "I suppose if you ask her nice, Mindy can take you to her secret lookout up on the rim."

Mindy blushed. "Pa, you know about my secret lookout?"

"I've known about it ever since you first started goin' there," Cap explained. "But I reckon ever'one ought to have 'em a place they can get off by themselves, now and again. I figured any time you went there you should be left alone."

Mindy walked around the table and kissed her father on the cheek.

"In case I never told you, no one could ever ask for a better pa," she said.

"You're not bad as a daughter, either," Cap answered. He cleared his throat. "But if we're finished tellin' each other how fine and dandy we are, there are a few things to be done yet. Why don't you show John to the lookout? Lonnie, you and me could start takin' supplies out to the rifle pits. I reckon bein' as we'll be eatin' breakfast out there in the mornin', we can take some of these biscuits, wrap 'em up in some cloth, and they'll do just fine."

"Sure thing, Cap," Lonnie replied.

John rode along behind Mindy as they climbed the trail to her lookout. It only took above five minutes of easy riding, and John calculated that the same distance could be covered in less than two if necessary. Once there, they dismounted, and John looked around.

Overhead, the stars glistened like diamonds and in the distance, Cap Rock Escarpment rose in a great and mysterious dark slab of earth and rock against the night sky. Down on the canyon floor the Locke herd stood motionless in rest. An owl landed nearby and his wings made a soft whirr as he flew by. He looked at John and Mindy with great round, glowing eyes.

"Well, this is it," Mindy said self-consciously. She moved her hand around in a sweeping gesture. "My secret hideaway."

"I can see why you like to come up here," John said. "It's really a nice place."

"It's a place where you can be alone and think," Mindy said.

A soft night breeze pushed across the glade and Mindy shivered once as it caressed her skin. There was a scent of wildflowers on the air.

"Cold?" John asked.

"No, I'm fine," Mindy replied, folding her arms across in front of her. "Is this place all right?"

"Yes, it'll be just the thing. I can see every approach from up here."

"I figure that when Scarns and his bunch come, they'll most likely come from that way," Mindy said, pointing south. "It's the easiest way in and if he thinks you're all alone out here, he won't be trying to sneak up on you."

"I think you're right," John agreed. He walked out to the edge of the precipice to look in the direction she had pointed. "I'm sure that from here I'll see them in plenty time to get back to the rest of you with the warning."

"John?"

There was something in Mindy's voice, a lonely, frightened sound. He turned to look back at her.

"John, it'll be all right, won't it? We will win, won't we?"

John smiled, trying to reassure her. "Yeah," he said. "We'll win."

"Why? Because we're right? I know that right is always supposed to win, but this is real life, this isn't some fairy tale."

"I suspect being right helps some," John said. He laughed quietly. "But probably not as much as your pa's Whitworth."

"You think that old cannon will really make a difference?"

"You forget, Mindy, your pa and I have seen what

a little well-aimed artillery can do to an advancing army." He laughed again. "The men in the artillery used to have a saying. Artillery lends dignity to what would otherwise be a common brawl."

Mindy laughed. After a moment she said, "John, do you know what I'm most frightened of?"

"What?"

"You and Pa have been in battles before. You were both in the War. I've never been. Oh, there've been the skirmishes when two or three men would ride out here and take potshots at us. But a full-scale battle? I just hope I don't do something to disgrace you, Pa, Lonnie, and myself."

John chuckled. "Mindy, you'll do fine. Believe me, when you've been around as long as I have, you can tell about something like that."

"I'll try my best," Mindy said. "I can promise you that. Now, since you are so good at predicting, tell me what's going to happen tomorrow."

"My guess is we'll stop them cold," John said. "After that it'll be all over. They won't try it again."

"John?"

"Yes?"

"After the fight's over tomorrow, you'll be leaving, won't you?"

John looked back out over the moon-silvered landscape. He was quiet for a long moment.

"You will, won't you?" Mindy asked again.

"Yes," he said.

"It's all right. I won't do anything, or say anything to try to stop you," Mindy promised.

John turned back toward her with a smile. "I reckon Lonnie will be glad to hear that."

"Thanks for not saying anything tonight."

"What do you mean? What would I have said?"

"I don't know," Mindy said. "Something, anything, I guess, that would have let them know. . ."

"Know what?" John asked. He came over and put his hands on Mindy's arms.

"Let them know I'm not the innocent girl they both think I am."

"Lord, girl, I've never known anyone more innocent," John said. He put his fingers to her cheek and felt a tear sliding down her face. "Just because you've become a woman, Mindy, that doesn't mean you aren't worth anything any more."

"It's all so confusing," Mindy said.

"There's no confusion to it. Trust me, I know what I'm talking about."

"Pa thinks I've set my cap for Lonnie."

"Have you?"

"I don't know. What if I had? How would you feel about it?"

"Mindy, there's one thing I want to know, and I want you to tell me the truth. You aren't just using Lonnie to get to me, are you?"

"No," Mindy said. She smiled. "I won't say I didn't think about it. Oh, John, I've thought it over. I don't love you . . . I mean, not like a woman loves a man she wants to marry. I just thought I loved you. We made love, and I thought that meant I had to love you."

John chuckled. "Well, you've not only become a woman, you've become a wise woman. What about Lonnie? What do you feel about him?"

"I don't know. I think I do see him in a different

way now. But I'm not ready to rush into something. I don't want to marry him just because I want to be married, or even..." She blushed and looked at the ground.

"Even what?"

"Even because I've discovered that I like being pleasured and it would be nice to have a husband so I could enjoy it any time I wanted."

"I'm glad you see it that way," John said. "Just let it be. If it's meant to happen, it will."

"I suppose I had better get back to the others," Mindy said. "They might start worrying about what happened to me."

"I suppose so."

"Are you going to spend the night up here on the rim?"

"Yes," John said.

"What about the rest of us? Where do you want us?"

"When you go back down, get the others in the rifle pits. Each of you take the same pits you had before so I'll know where you are. Leave the pit with the dynamite fuses for me. When I see them coming, I'll come down and warn you all to get ready. You got that?"

"Yes," Mindy said.

"After I let you know they're on the way, I'm coming back up here to wait on them. I'll stay here until they are well in range. Then I'll open up on them, and that will be the signal to fire. With the crossfire effect, the dynamite, and the six-pounder, we'll cut them to pieces."

"There's going to be a lot of blood shed tomorrow, isn't there?"

"Yes," John said. "But with any luck, none of it will be ours."

"Oh, John, I have the strangest feeling."

"What kind of feeling?"

"I can't explain it, but it's almost a feeling of exhilaration. Isn't that awful? I know there's going to be a terrible battle tomorrow, but now I'm actually beginning to look forward to it. How can that be?"

"You're just getting a taste of what war is all about, that's all," John said. "Men talk about how terrible war is, and there's always fear the night before a battle. But there's another side to it too, a darker side. There's something inside humans that makes them crave battle."

"Have you ever felt that exhilaration?"

"Of course," John admitted. "But if it's used properly, it's not necessarily a bad thing," he went on. "It can give a person courage. If I didn't have that side of me to call on from time to time, I wouldn't be around."

"Do you . . . do you feel it when you're in a gunfight?"

"Yes. At least, I feel enough of it to see me through," John said. "It's like anything else; a person has to know when to use it, and when to walk away. Folks that crave the feeling all the time find it real easy to turn killer."

"Like Preacher Jack?"

"I reckon that was part of it," John admitted.

"I wouldn't want too much of it," Mindy said.

John laughed. "Don't reckon you'll have to be worrying about that."

Mindy kissed John on the mouth. Her lips were cool, and the kiss was controlled. She pulled away from him and smiled at him.

"It wouldn't take much, John Slocum, for me to tell you a real goodbye, the kind we could both think about all night. But I reckon that wouldn't be the right thing to do just now."

"I reckon not," John admitted reluctantly.

Mindy turned and walked back to her horse. She mounted, then looked back at him.

"Like my pa has always said, you're a good man, John Slocum." She laughed, then added in a low, sultry voice, "He just doesn't know how good a man you really are."

She clucked at her horse, and John watched her ride back down the trail until she was gone. He found himself thinking about a red dirt farm in Georgia. If things had been different, if he could relive his life, Mindy or a girl like her would certainly have a place in it.

"Yeah," he said aloud in a disgusted voice which showed his anger with himself for allowing such thoughts to slip in. "And if a frog had wings he wouldn't bump his ass every time he jumps."

Mindy found her father by the Whitworth gun, laying out powder and shell. The barrel of the gun glistened softly in the moonlight.

"You get John set up?" Cap asked as he worked to stack the ammunition near the piece.

"Yes," Mindy said.

"What do you think of my little beauty here?" Cap asked, patting the barrel lovingly.

"Pa, are you sure you can do this all by yourself? I thought it took a whole lot of people to shoot off one of these things?"

"No problem, daughter. This here is a breech loader."

"What difference does that make?"

"Well, it makes all the difference in the world," Cap explained. He twisted the breech handle, then opened the block at the rear end of the gun. "You see," he went on, "with most cannons you have to run powder from the south of the barrel, then poke a ball down, then shoot. After each shot you have to sponge down the barrel to make sure there's no burning pieces of powder left to fire off your next load before you're ready. That takes a whole crew—a loader, sponger, vent man, aimer, and gun captain."

"And this one isn't that way?"

"Oh, no. With this one, all I have to do is push a shell in through the back, like this." He demonstrated. "Then put one of the little bags of powder behind it like this, close the block, and yank on this cord. It's as easy as shootin' a rifle."

"You're looking forward to it, aren't you, Pa?"

Cap patted the barrel of the gun again and chuckled. "Well now, maybe I am a little," he admitted. "But don't forget, daughter, I didn't have nothin' to do with startin' this. That was all Scarns's doin'."

"I know," Mindy said. She sighed. "Tomorrow it'll be all over."

"You ain't worried, are you, daughter?"

"No," Mindy said. "I really do feel that we will win."

"Then why do you sound so upset that it'll all be over tomorrow?"

"You know, Pa, that John will be leaving when it's finished?"

"Never figured on anythin' any different," Cap said easily.

"I thought . . . that is, I hoped he'd stay around for a while."

"John ain't that kind," Cap said. "He's always been one with wanderin' feet. You'd hear about him in Wyoming, then Colorado, then someone would say no, they seen him in Kansas, and the next thing you know you'd find out he was in California."

"You think he'll ever settle down?"

Cap chuckled. "Sure, some day; when they plant him six feet under."

"Not before? You don't think he'll ever take up with a woman, maybe start a family?"

"No, I can't see John doin'—" Cap paused in mid-sentence and studied his daughter. "See here, girl, are you tryin' to tell me somethin'?"

"What?"

"Are you and John . . ."

Mindy laughed. "Pa, don't sound like an irate father!" she said. "John is a perfect gentleman."

"That's good," Cap said.

"I was just curious, that's all."

"Before you get too curious about a man, make sure it's someone that'll be likely to settle down and run a ranch," Cap suggested. "You might find that you don't have to look too far."

"You're talking about Lonnie?"

"Lonnie's a good man," Cap said.

"He is," Mindy agreed.

"The way you was carryin' on at the supper table, I thought you'd already made up your mind."

"Not yet, Pa. I need a little time."

"You ain't gonna find me rushin' you into anything," Cap said. "Whatever you want is fine with me."

"Thanks, Pa," Mindy said, kissing him on the cheek. "A girl couldn't ask for a more understanding father."

15

The piano was playing merrily, but the noise in the saloon was such that no one could hear it from more than ten feet away. In one corner a group of raucous men had started their own singing in competition with the piano. One of those men, Tom Mahoney noticed, was Fergus Gant. He thought Gant seemed in fine spirits for one who came so close to getting killed today.

Tucker Scarns stepped up to the bar.

"Hello, Scarns," Tom said. "You want a beer?"

"Yeah, Mahoney, if it ain't too green," Scarns ordered.

Mahoney ladled the beer from a clay *olla* that kept it cool, leaving a small head on it, and handed the full mug to Scarns. Scarns blew off the suds, then took his first drink, while Mahoney went back to rubbing his rag on the bar. If asked, Mahoney would have said he was cleaning the bar. In reality he was just spreading the spilt liquor around, which did nothing toward improving the bar surface.

There was a commotion on the floor, then a loud burst of laughter, and Scarns turned around and leaned back against the bar to watch. One of the men had shoved several tables aside and was doing his interpretation of the Mexican Hat Dance.

"Hey, Dusty!" Gant called to the dancer. "What are you tryin' to do? Learn to dance the fandango?"

"He'll never do it," Morgan laughed. "Hell, he can't dance any better'n he can punch cows."

"Never said I could punch cows," Dusty shouted. "That's why I sell my guns."

Dusty jumped up and attempted to kick his heels together, but his spurs got tangled and he fell to the floor in a heap. His fall was greeted with loud laughter and Gant tossed him a bottle. Dusty turned the bottle up and took several deep swallows while still seated on the floor.

Scarns laughed, along with the others.

"Hey, are you gonna just sit there on the floor suckin' on that bottle like a baby on a sugar tittie, or are we goin' upstairs and get us a real tit to suck on?" Gant called.

Dusty pulled himself up. "We're goin' upstairs," he said, and, unsteadily, he started toward the stairs which led to the second-floor whorehouse.

Scarns drained his mug, then turned around and pushed it toward Mahoney.

"Again," he ordered.

"Your men seem to be in uncommon good

spirits," Mahoney said as he pulled the dipper from the *olla,* ladled the mug full again. Evaporation kept the beer reasonably cool.

"Why not?" Scarns asked. "By tomorrow this war will be over. They'll be paid off and I'll have the Lazy L."

"And you think that's a good thing, do you?" Mahoney asked, pushing the full mug toward Scarns.

Scarns looked at Mahoney for a moment, and his eyes flashed anger.

"You sayin' it *ain't* a good thing?"

"Seems to me like the valley ought to be big enough for you and Locke both," Mahoney said. "It was good and peaceful 'round here till you started the war."

"Locke had the water. It ain't right, one man havin' all the water."

"He didn't have the water until he dug the channel for it," Mahoney said. "You coulda done the same thing for the Box S."

"Maybe I could and maybe I couldn't. Why should I bother if Locke already did the job for me? All I need is to take over his land."

"So you start a range war," Mahoney said.

"There ain't nothin' new about that," Scarns defended. "What's the difference between a range war and any other kind of war? Shit, it was a war that stole Texas from the Mexicans, wasn't it? And most of the West was took from the Indians. You think it matters whether wars are fought by countries or by men? It's the same thing. A country wants more land, it starts a war and takes it. And a country ain't nothin' but men in the first place. Only then it's called patriotism."

"And you figure it is patriotism that's makin' you steal Locke's land?"

"From what I hear, Locke may be dead. That new gunhand he hired is takin' over. Hell, he's a johnny-come-lately. Bein' as I been here longer, surely I got more right to Locke's land than he does."

"Slocum may have somethin' to say about that," Mahoney suggested.

"He's all alone," Scarns replied. "There ain't a whole lot he can say. 'Specially after me and my men pay him a call tomorrow."

"You're plannin' to ride out there with near twenty men and kill him?"

"Or run him off," Scarns said. "Whatever it takes."

"That ain't right," Mahoney said.

"What the hell do you know about right?" Scarns asked. "How do you think Charlie Goodnight got where he is? He just rode into the Palo Duro Canyon and took it over. He drove out the Comanches who were livin' there, run off the few homesteaders he found, and kilt off all the buffalo. Now folks say Charlie Goodnight is a great man. Well, mark my words, Mahoney, one of these days they'll be sayin' that about me." Scarns took several swallows of his beer, then wiped the back of his hand across his mouth. "Yes, sir," he said. "In the same breath as they talk about Jesse Chisholm and Charlie Goodnight they'll be sayin' Tucker Scarns. Soon as I take care of Mr. Slocum."

"Or he takes care of you," Mahoney suggested.

Scarns's eyes narrowed angrily and he looked at the barkeep. "You'd like that wouldn't you, Mahoney?"

"I don't aim to take sides in this here battle," Mahoney said.

"Seems to me you already have."

"Not true. I don't aim to ride out there with you, and I don't aim to be out there to help Slocum. Either way it comes out is fine with me."

"Either way is fine, you say?" Scarns said. "Tell you what, Mahoney. Don't you be here when I come back."

"What do you mean? Where would I go?"

"I don't care where you go, as long as it's away from here."

"This here is my saloon, Scarns," Mahoney said. "I don't aim to leave it."

"I'm buyin' it," Scarns said.

"I ain't sellin'."

"I think you are," Scarns said. "Leave your forwardin' address. I'm buyin' it for two hundred dollars."

"Two hundred dollars? It's worth more than that."

"Two hundred dollars and not a penny more. I'll send you the money."

"I ain't leavin'," Mahoney insisted.

Scarns smiled without mirth.

"Oh, you're leavin' all right, one way or the other. If I see your ugly face behind this bar when I come back tomorrow, I'll kill you." His smile broadened. "And I'll find some way to make it legal. I can do that, 'cause I'll be the law by then."

Scarns downed the rest of his beer, then walked angrily over to the batwings, pushed them open, and went out onto the boardwalk. He stood there for a moment letting the breeze cool him, then he started walking down toward the end of the street.

The tinkling sound of the piano fell off behind him until soon it was barely audible. Now the sounds he heard were from natural sources: the brushy whisper of a tumbleweed being pushed before a gentle breeze, frogs and crickets serenading in the dark, the far-off bark of a coyote, the leathery whick of bullbats' wings as they windmilled overhead after insects.

Scarns leaned on the fence of the corral at the edge of town and looked north toward the Lazy L. He couldn't see anything from here, but he knew it was out there and he knew that Slocum was there waiting for him.

Scarns heard a sound behind him and he jerked around quickly, his pistol already in his hand.

"Easy, Tucker, easy," a woman's sultry voice said.

"Kate," Scarns said, recognizing the girl from the saloon. "I figured you'd be busy tonight."

Kate chuckled. "I must say your men are making a night of it. But the other girls seem to be handling the situation just fine."

"What are you doing out here?"

"You got poor old Tom all nervous and upset," Kate said. "What with your talk of forcin' him to sell out."

"Mahoney needs to learn a little loyalty," Scarns said. "That's all."

"Aw, now, honey, you know that he has to be neutral in all things," Kate said. "A man who serves the public can't afford to be any other way. If it's any consolation to you, he'd probably have made Cap Locke just as mad if he came in here tonight. Or John Slocum. He's not against you, honey, you know that."

Scarns rubbed his cheek and looked at her. He smiled. "You sure seem to be arguing his case for him," he said. "He send you out here?"

"Yes," Kate lied. She thrust out a hip provocatively, and smiled at him. "He said, 'Kate, honey, you go out there and calm Mr. Scarns down.'"

"Did he tell you how to do that?" Scarns asked. His tongue grew thick and his voice a little strained. He felt a shortness of breath, and a pressure in his pants.

Kate knew what she was doing to him and she stepped up close enough to reach him. She put her hand down on the bulge in his pants. "He told me to do whatever it takes," she said. "What, exactly, is it going to take?" she asked.

"What do you care what happens to him?" Scarns asked.

"Why, honey, he's my husband," Kate said sweetly.

"Your . . . your husband?" he asked. "Well, if you want your husband to keep his saloon, don't play around. You do what pleases me."

Later, Scarns was leaning against the corral fence trying to catch his breath, recover his strength. He looked over at Kate, who was standing quietly beside him.

"Tell him," he said. "He can stay."

"I thought you'd see things my way," Kate said, smiling sweetly. "Now, if you will excuse me, I'll go help out the other girls. Your men are so horny you'd think this was their last night on earth."

The impact of what she said didn't hit Scarns until Kate was already back down to the saloon.

• • •

Marcus Dunne heard a loud banging and he turned over in his bed, thinking it was just a dream and would soon go away.

"Dunne! Dunne, open up this here store!"

"Marcus," Dunne's wife said, shaking him. "Marcus, there is someone downstairs, banging on the front door."

Marcus Dunne, who lived in an apartment over the general store, grunted once.

"Dunne! Open up this here store or I'm gonna kick in the door!"

"Marcus, wake up, I say! Someone is downstairs!"

By now Dunne was fully awake and he sat up in bed. He could hear the banging on the front door quite clearly now.

"What the hell?" he said. "What time is it?"

"I heard the clock strike two a short while ago," his wife answered.

"Two? Two in the morning?"

Again came the insistent banging on the front door. Dunne got out of bed and shuffled, barefoot, across the wide board floor. He pushed up the window sash.

"What do you want?" he called down.

"I want you to open up the store."

"What? Are you crazy? It's two o'clock in the mornin'. Who the hell are you, anyway?"

"Tucker Scarns."

Dunne gasped. He paused for just a second, then he yelled back down, "Right away, Mr. Scarns. I'm comin' right away."

"Are you crazy?" his wife asked, when Dunne lit

a lantern. "Are you really going to open the store now?"

"I don't aim to tell Tucker Scarns no," Dunne said nervously. He pulled on a pair of pants but left on his nightshirt, sticking the tail of it down into the pants.

A golden bubble of light followed Dunne down the stairs, then through the dark shadows of the store. He opened the front door and saw Tucker Scarns standing on the porch.

"It took you long enough," Scarns growled, pushing his way into the store.

"I'm sorry," Dunne said. "It's not often I get a customer at this time of day. What . . . what can I do for you, Mr. Scarns?"

"You still got that fancy coffin in the back? The black one with the silverwork on it that you showed me before?"

"The 'Eternal Cloud,' you mean? Yes, sir, I got it," Dunne said.

"How much is it?"

"Why, I believe it's . . . a hunnert and fifty dollars," Dunne said, quickly adding fifty dollars to its actual retail price.

Scarns pulled out his billfold and counted out the money. He handed the bills to Dunne. "I'll take it."

"You've just bought yourself a fine coffin, Mr. Scarns. Where do you want it delivered?"

"Right there," Scarns said, pointing to the front window of the store.

"I beg your pardon?"

"Right there," Scarns said again. "I want you to move all that stuff out of the window—the boots, the shirts, the saddle. Move it all out of the window and put the coffin there."

"But why would you want to do that?"

"'Cause they's a body gonna be lyin' in it, that's why," Scarns said. "I want it propped up so's the people in the town can walk by and see it. And I want you to paint a sign and put it above the coffin."

"What do you want on the sign?"

"Celebrated gunfighter, John Slocum, killed by Tucker Scarns in a fair fight."

Dunne gasped. "You . . . you killed John Slocum?"

"Not yet, I ain't," Scarns said. "But I'll have the deed done before noon, and I'll bring the body to you. You have this ready for it." He peeled off another twenty dollars. "Here, find somethin' presentable for him to be buried in. He'll like as not have on a shirt and denim trousers. He's my trophy, I want him dressed proper."

"Yes, sir," Dunne said, smiling broadly. It was beginning to turn into a profitable night. He would wake up at two o'clock every morning for this kind of money.

16

At four o'clock in the morning Tucker Scarns began gathering his men for the attack on the Lazy L Ranch. He pulled them from the whorehouse and out of the saloon. Some he found passed out on the ground outside, and one was lying in a water trough.

When he gathered them all together he noticed that Fergus Gant was gone. Morgan said he had ridden out in the middle of the night after declaring that he had no intention of facing Slocum again. Well, let him go, Scarns thought. He had no time for someone as yellow-livered as that. This was a job for men, and if you couldn't be a man, you had no business getting involved.

As they rode through the pre-dawn darkness toward the Lazy L Ranch, Scarns looked around at the riders who composed his army. Morgan and Dusty were pretty good boys; they had worked for him since he arrived. The others were drifters, hired just for their guns. They had been a drain on him since he hired them. None of them were worth a damn when there was real work to be done. He would be glad to be rid of them once this was over.

As he looked at them now, bleary-eyed and weaving in the saddle as they rode, he was beginning to wonder if they would be any good even for what he had hired them for. They were certainly a motley crew. The ones who weren't drunk were hung over. It was scarcely an army one would lead into a real battle. On the other hand, it certainly should be enough of an army to handle one man, even if that man was John Slocum.

Scarns shifted his position to take a little pressure off his groin. Kate had worked his knob over so well last night that he felt as if he had been put through a vise. He'd been in whorehouses from Mexico to Missouri, but he'd never had anything like that.

Scarns hadn't slept a wink, but he wasn't even tired. The only thing he was feeling was a sense of excitement. In a little over an hour it would all be over, and he would be in control of the entire valley.

The first thing he was going to do was fire all the deadwood that had been collecting around his place, and replace them with workers . . . real workers.

Fred Stone had been a real worker. He was a good, dependable hand, and that bastard Preacher Jack had killed him. Scarns had talked to Preacher Jack about it afterwards, but Preacher Jack didn't seem to understand what Scarns was saying. He had

a feeling Preacher Jack wasn't one who would have
been willing just to take his money and leave.
Preacher Jack might have wanted to stay on for a
while, even if Scarns didn't want him. Scarns was
glad the son of a bitch was dead. He didn't need him,
or anyone like him.

Or did he?

Scarns thought about that for a while. If he were
king of the roost, what would keep someone from
coming along and knocking him off the hill? That
was the way things were done out here. Whoever
won was a winner only as long as he could hold onto
his winnings. Well, by God, he was going to hold
onto them, and he didn't need any uncontrollable
bastards like Preacher Jack to help him, either. He
could set it up himself, use men he knew and trusted.
King of the hill. A child's game. Maybe a man's
game, too, when you got right down to it.

"Morgan," Scarns called.

The wiry young rider pulled up alongside.

"You want me?"

"I been thinkin'. Once I get control of things
around here, I'm gonna have to keep me a private
army just to make sure I stay in control. You know
what I mean?"

"Yeah, I know what you mean."

"How'd you like to be the head of that army?"

"Me? Are you serious? I can be the head of your
army?"

"Under me, of course," Scarns reminded him.

"Well, sure, under you. I know that."

"What do you say?"

"I say yeah, I'd like that," Morgan said. He
smiled. "I'd like that a lot. Only thing is, what would

the law say about you runnin' a private army?"

"I got that all figured out. I'll get Sixgun incorporated, set myself up as mayor," Scarns explained. "I'll make you the marshal. You can have as many deputies as you need. That way it'll all be legal."

"You ain't expectin' me to do all this for what you're payin' me now, are you?"

"Oh, I think there will be more in it than that," Scarns said. "All we have to do is pass a law to raise some taxes. After all, you'll be a public servant, so the public should pay you."

"Yeah," Morgan said. "The public should pay me." He laughed.

"If we play our cards right, we can make the army profitable for all concerned," Scarns said.

"Tell me, Scarns, when you get rich, you gonna hobnob with all them other rich folk, like Goodnight and Chisholm and Kohrs?"

"Any reason why I shouldn't?" Scarns replied.

"No reason I can think of," Morgan said. " 'Ceptin' the fact that you'll have to get all decked out in one of them suits and ties." Morgan put his finger to his collar and pulled it away as if he were wearing a tie.

"I'm aware of that," Scarns said.

"And you're willin' to do it?" Morgan asked.

"Yes. Why not?"

"You ain't never gonna catch me in one of them chokin' outfits. Wearin' a tie would be just like havin' a rope around your neck."

"That's the difference between us, Morgan. I'm a man of ambition and responsibility. I'm willin' to use any means to get there, but once I'm there, I intend to leave all this behind and become as respectable as anyone in the state. For me, the end justifies the means. For you, the means is the end."

Morgan laughed. "I'm not sure what the hell you're talkin' about, but if that means I don't ever have to put on one of them dandy suits, then you're right," he said. "But it ain't true that I got no ambition. I got plenty of ambition."

"Tell me, Morgan. What is your ambition?"

"Once I got me that position of power I want a free ticket to screw ever' whore between here and Amarillo."

"A noble ambition, to be sure," Scarns replied sarcastically, but his sarcasm was lost on Morgan.

"The Lazy L is just over the next hill," Morgan pointed out.

"Yeah, I know. We'll stop here until dawn."

Slocum was on the rim of the canyon waiting for them. Years of living on the trail, surviving by wits and instinct, had taught Slocum the trick of being alert even while asleep. He knew that staying awake the entire night would dull his edge, yet he couldn't sleep so soundly that Scarns and his men would be able to ride right in without being observed. Therefore he took a series of catnaps, dozing for five minutes out of every ten.

When Scarns's men came into range, he awakened sharply, a scent of danger in his nostrils, his skin tingling in anticipation. It was just before dawn; a tiny sliver of pink streaked across the eastern horizon. He moved out onto the rim and looked toward the south in the direction Mindy had indicated they would come from. There, he saw Scarns and his men, moving like shadows through the sage.

Behind Slocum his horse was ready to ride, ground-tied in a tiny draw. He slipped back to the horse, then mounted and urged it back down the draw. He moved as quickly as he could without breaking into a gallop, which would alert Scarns and his men.

Lonnie was the first to greet him when he reached the line of defenses.

"Have you seen anything?" Lonnie asked anxiously.

"They're coming," Slocum said calmly.

"Good," Lonnie replied. He flexed his hands nervously against his rifle. "I'm ready for 'em, Mr. Slocum. I say let's do it and show 'em what for."

"Where are the others?"

"Same place as you told us to be. Mindy's in that pit right over there. Cap, he's back on the high ground with his cannon."

"I'm going to go tell them to be ready," John said. "Now, remember, don't open fire until I give the signal."

"What will the signal be?"

John smiled. "Don't worry, you won't miss it."

"All right," Lonnie said. "I'll be ready."

Slocum ran, crouched over, to the pit where Mindy waited. "Mindy?" he said softly.

"Here, John."

"They're on the way."

"How long before they get here?"

"No more than ten minutes," John said.

Mindy looked toward the east. "That means it'll be full light by the time they arrive."

"Yeah, I'm sure they timed it that way. That's all

right, it'll just make them easier targets for us. How do you feel?"

"I feel fine. I'm ready," Mindy said. Then she added, "I guess."

John smiled at her. "Don't worry, Mindy. You'll do us all proud." He started back toward the Whitworth.

"John?"

John looked back at her. She had never looked more beautiful, or more vulnerable, than at this moment, and he cursed the fates that put her here, in a rifle pit, waiting to do battle with an attacking army.

"I'm glad you're here with us," she said.

"Hell," John quipped, "what else have I got to do?"

Cap was polishing the barrel of his Whitworth when John reached him.

"You're going to polish right through that thing," John cautioned him.

"Just because it's a machine of war doesn't mean it can't be kept lookin' pretty," Cap said proudly. "When this is all over I'm goin' to keep it on display in my front yard. It'll serve two purposes: it'll scare people off, and I think it'll look damn fine."

"Oh, I'm sure it will."

"What's up?" Cap asked.

"They're here," John said simply.

"Good," Cap said. "I been waitin' for this moment a long time." He opened the breechblock and slid in a shell, then loaded a bag of powder behind it. He closed the block, then patted the gun.

"Everything all set?" John asked.

"Let 'em come," Cap said simply.

John started back, but Cap called out to him.

"Yes?" John asked.

Cap pointed back toward the barn. "What about the line riders, John? They're still anxious to help out."

"I don't know. I'd just as soon they not get in it."

"I wish you'd find somethin' for them," Cap said. "Maybe we don't need it, but I think they do. They have somethin' to prove to themselves, and I aim to keep 'em on after this is all over. I'd like for 'em to feel good about it."

"All right. I'll go back to see them," John promised. "They can move around into a blocking position to keep Scarns and the others from getting away."

"Thanks, John. They'll appreciate that," Cap said.

When John told the line riders that Scarns was here, and gave them the opportunity to move into position to block any escape attempt, the riders thanked him profusely.

"You're sure you want to get involved?" John asked.

"We've talked about it some," Jimmy explained. "The way we look at it, cowboyin' is what we do for a livin'. If Cap gets run off, there won't be nobody left to ride for around here 'ceptin' Tucker Scarns. And there ain't none of us too keen on ridin' for that son of a bitch."

John grinned. "Sounds like reason enough to me," he said. "When we start shooting we're gonna open up with everything we got. That's rifles, dynamite, and Cap's Whitworth. That's gonna surprise Scarns and his men pretty good, and some of 'em might try to get away. That's where you'll come in."

"Believe me, they ain't none of 'em gonna get away," Jimmy promised. "Right, boys?"

"Right," they answered.

"All right," Slocum said. "Get mounted and get yourselves in position. This ball is going to open soon."

Jimmy and the line riders mounted, then left, circling wide so as to get into position to block Scarns's escape without being seen.

John remounted, then rode back out to the canyon rim to wait the final few minutes.

It was light now, the soft gray of early dawn. Scarns and the others were riding up slowly, still spread wide, still moving quietly. They rode up close to the ranch house, then Scarns held up his hand in a signal to halt. They stopped and stood like a row of statues, looking at the house, searching for any sign of life.

John eased up onto the rim a bit and looked back down toward Lonnie's pit. He saw the young man in position, holding his rifle at the ready. John raised his finger to his lips in a sign to keep quiet, then he pointed toward Mindy's pit and indicated that Lonnie should pass the signal along.

Lonnie nodded, and passed the signal to Mindy, who passed it on to her father. The four were absolutely quiet, totally still, as Scarns and his men surveyed the house.

"There don't seem to be no one around," Morgan Cole said. His voice carried well in the still dawn, and John and the others could hear every word.

"You don't reckon the old man died and Slocum

turned yellow and run, do you?" Dusty asked.

"I've heard a lot of words about Slocum," Scarns said, "but yellow ain't never been one of them. Morgan, send a man up there to give the house a look-see."

"Shorty," Morgan directed, "go on up, have a look around."

The rider Morgan hailed slapped his heels against the side of his horse, then urged the animal up toward the quiet house. He cocked his rifle as he approached, and held it across his saddle at the ready. He stopped about fifteen yards away from the front porch.

"Hello the house!" he called. "Anyone in there?"

Shorty sat on his horse for a long moment, waiting for an answer. When no one responded he looked back toward Scarns and the others.

Scarns indicated by hand signals that Shorty should dismount and have a closer look. Shorty swung down and, carrying his rifle at the ready, walked up onto the porch. He knocked on the door.

"Slocum!" he called. "Slocum, you in there?"

When Shorty got no answer, he walked over to the window and looked in. After that, he hopped down off the porch and walked all the way around the house, peering in every window. He reappeared from the back side.

"Ain't nobody here!" he yelled.

"Go on inside!" Scarns shouted back to him. "Make sure!"

Shorty leaned his rifle against the wall of the house and pulled his pistol, then pushed the door open and stepped inside. Scarns and the others waited quietly for a few moments. Then Shorty reappeared on the back porch, waving both arms.

"Son of a bitch!" Morgan said. "He musta pulled out."

"What do we do now?" Dusty asked.

"Let's go in, move those cattle out of the corrals," Scarns ordered. "Case they come back, they can just fret on that for a while. Morgan, you make a wide circle, see if there's anything we ought to know about. The rest of you men stay ready. If it's a trick and you see any Lazy L riders, you blow 'em out of their saddles."

The Box S riders came in slow, passed Lonnie and Mindy on their flanks, heading straight for Cap's gun position on the high ground. Slocum slipped backwards over the canyon rim and climbed back into the saddle. He counted to ten, then buried his long spurs deep into his horse's tender flanks. He sailed over the rim, daylight showing between his butt and the saddle, charging straight for the man on the far edge of Scarns's flank.

"Now!" he shouted, bringing his rifle up to fire.

17

When the first light of day splashed in through the door of the saloon, Tom Maloney was sitting morosely at one of the tables drinking his own whiskey. Tom had learned long ago that bartenders who drink heavily have short careers. It was, therefore, most unusual for him to be drunk, but drunk he was.

Kate walked heavily out onto the balcony which overlooked the saloon floor. She saw Tom sitting at the table, the bottle before him nearly empty, his glass nearly full.

"Tom," she called down.

Tom looked up, said nothing, looked back down, and took another drink.

Kate pulled her robe around her shoulders, then walked stiffly down the stairs. She'd been whoring for five years and the only time she'd ever had a night like last night was up in Colorado right after a gold strike. That was where she met and married Tom Maloney.

"Tom," she said again when she reached the table, "what's wrong?"

"You know what's wrong," Tom said.

Kate sat down across the table from him. "Is it about last night? Because I helped the girls? It was your idea that I wouldn't come off the line for three more years. We agreed that I would stay at it until we were comfortably fixed."

"No," Tom said, "that ain't it."

"What is it, then? Scarns? Because I did it with Scarns?"

"Yeah."

Kate put her hand on Tom's arm. "Honey, why is it any different with Scarns than with any other man? None of them mean anything to me. You know that."

"That ain't it," Tom said. He took a deep breath. "It's . . . it's that you did it to save my skin. I didn't ask you to, but I know why you went out there to him."

"Well, honey, that's not bad. That's just good sense," Kate said. "I'm glad I did it. I don't want to lose everything we've got here, and I don't want to lose you."

Tom got up and walked over to the door, then looked out onto the quiet street. He saw something in the front window of the general store and he stared at it. "What the hell?" he said.

"What is it?" Kate asked.

"What's that damnfool Dunne got in his front window?" Tom asked. He pushed through the batwings and walked across the street. Dunne was sweeping his front porch, raising the dust with his broom.

"Good morning, Tom," Dunne said brightly. "It's awful early in the morning for you to be up, ain't it? I know I wouldn't be, if I hadn't done some business in the middle of the night."

Tom didn't answer. Instead, he stood on the board sidewalk looking at the shining black coffin which was propped up in the window and reading the sign above it.

> HERE LIES THE CELEBRATED
> GUNFIGHTER
> JOHN SLOCUM
> KILLED IN A FAIR FIGHT
> BY TUCKER SCARNS

"Dunne, what the hell is this?" Tom asked. "There's no one in that coffin."

"Not yet," Dunne answered. "But I suspect there soon will be. I imagine there will be several other coffins filled as well. I certainly hope I have enough to accommodate everyone." Dunne began to whistle a happy tune.

"Why have you got Slocum's name there?"

"Why, Mr. Scarns bought the coffin last night," Dunne replied. "It's on his instructions that I put that sign there."

"Get it down."

"No, sir, I can't do that," Dunne explained.

"Damn it, I said take that sign down!"

"And I said I can't do that," Dunne replied.

Tom saw a large rock on the ground by the corner

of the porch. He reached down and picked it up, and before Dunne could stop him, threw it through the front window. The window exploded with a loud, tinkling crash. One long shard of glass dangled for a moment, then it too fell.

"My God, are you crazy?" Dunne asked, putting his hands to his head. "What are you doing?"

"I've taken all I'm going to take from Mr. Tucker Scarns," Tom said. "He bought this coffin, so the sign over it will be his."

"You can't do that," Dunne said.

Tom looked at Dunne with a fierce glare. "Try and stop me," he challenged, as he pulled down the sign Dunne had put up. Tom flipped it over. "Where's the paintbrush you used?"

"Please, Tom! If Scarns comes back and finds that sign down, he'll kill me. I don't know what I could do to stop him."

The expression on Tom's face softened for a moment then hardened again. "I know what I did," he said without explanation. "At least I let it happen. But, by God, I'll never let a woman . . ."

"What do you mean?"

"Never mind." Tom saw the paintbrush and can in the corner of the window shelf.

A few moments later Tom put a new sign over the coffin:

TUCKER SCARNS
A THIEF, A CHEAT, AND A COWARD
THIS SIGN PAINTED BY TOM MALONEY

"Leave the sign up, Dunne," Tom ordered, "or you won't have to worry about Tucker Scarns."

"All right," Dunne agreed fearfully. "But if Tucker Scarns comes back, I'm going to show him your name on the sign. And you owe me for a new window."

"Put it on my bill," Tom said as he walked back across the street. He felt a hell of a lot better now than he had when the sun came up.

Slocum snapped off a shot, firing his rifle from the hip. A Box S rider dropped from the saddle and all hell broke loose.

"It's Slocum!" Morgan shouted. "He's back here!"

Scarns's men scattered, frightened and surprised by Slocum's sudden appearance. They fired at him as he zigzagged through their ranks, but their aim was totally ineffective.

Lonnie opened fire then and a new rider tumbled from his saddle.

"What the hell? Where did that come from?" Dusty shouted in surprise.

"Everybody get under cover over there," Morgan called, pointing toward a mound that looked as if it would offer some protection. The riders started toward the mound, but Mindy eased her rifle over the parapet and fired, dropping the nearest rider.

"Son of a bitch! He's got men there too!" Scarns shouted, and his men wheeled again, this time bent on leaving the way they rode in.

Slocum waved his rifle over his head and Brad, Jimmy, and another line rider came galloping up, guns blazing. Scarns's escape route was slammed shut.

Slocum took out the wide man, then headed for the bunker where the fuses to all the dynamite charges terminated. Out of the corner of his eye he saw one of the line riders go down.

Morgan found six men who hadn't yet been committed to the battle. He rallied them and they started charging toward Mindy's bunker.

"They ain't nothin' but one little ol' girl in that bunker!" Morgan shouted. "Come on! You gonna let a girl turn you back?"

Slocum looked around toward Cap and gave him the signal. Cap jerked on the lanyard. There was a flash of light and a puff of smoke. The Whitworth rocked back on its wheels as the heavy, stomach-jarring explosion rolled across the ground toward John.

The six-pound shell exploded in the middle of the group of riders Morgan was leading. Smoke, dirt, and dust wiped them out for a moment. Then they emerged from the cloud fewer in number than when they went in. Morgan was one of those who went down.

"Goddamn! They got a cannon!" Dusty shouted.

The shock of that discovery halted everyone in their tracks for a moment and they milled around in confusion.

Working quickly, Cap loaded another round, jerked the lanyard, and sent another shell flying into another group of men, doing terrible damage.

"Spread out! Spread out!" Scarns called. "He can't get us all with that cannon!"

Cap fired a third time, and this time the shell exploded harmlessly, Scarns's warning having done its job of dispersing the men.

"We've got them now!" Scarns shouted. "Hell, there can't be more than three or four of them!"

John knew he would have to go for broke now. Scarns wanted it all and as long as he was alive, he would try to drive Cap off the land. There was no turning back now. This was war, total and complete.

John lit the fuses one at a time. He listened to them hiss as they burned, watched the little trail of sparkling fire race across the ground toward the bundles of dynamite.

The charges were placed across the field like a fan. Scarns had spread his remaining men to avoid the artillery, but John was counting on the placement of the charges to be so thorough that he would be able to stop them.

The earth erupted in a series of horrendous explosions. Men and horses flew through the air and John saw the sickening sight of several large chunks of flesh taking wing.

The shock effect halted the troops in their tracks. They drifted together and Cap fired the Whitworth again, taking out another three men.

John raised up and fired his rifle. From the corner of his eye he saw Lonnie and Mindy do the same thing. From the back the two line riders, Jimmy and Brad, were pouring in their own fire. The Box S riders were caught in a devastating crossfire and they crumpled under the bullets, going down one by one.

Scarns looked around in total shock. He had come out here expecting Slocum to give up, or at the most to put up an ineffectual defense. He wasn't prepared to fight a full-scale war, and he certainly didn't expect the carnage which was unfolding before him.

Morgan was dead, killed by the first round from the cannon. Dusty was down, shot from his saddle by the deadly accurate rifle fire. Shorty was taken out, along with half a dozen others, by the dynamite charges. It was all over now. There was nothing left for him. His army, his dream, were all gone.

"Goddamn you, Slocum!" Scarns shouted. "Goddamn you all to hell!"

Scarns spurred his horse and started racing across the open field in an effort to escape. Lonnie raised up and fired at him, but missed. Mindy tried, only to discover that she was out of ammunition. Cap sent a six-pound shell whistling toward him but the hurtling round, black against an early morning cloudbank, passed over Scarns's head and exploded harmlessly in a stand of cedar trees five hundred yards away.

"He's getting away, John!" Cap shouted. "The son of a bitch is getting away!"

John saw where Scarns was headed, then he smiled. He touched off the last fuse, then stepped up onto the parapet with his arms crossed, watching almost casually as the little trail of golden sparks raced across the ground. The fuse passed under Scarns's galloping horse, then, a second later, erupted in a huge blast. Scarns had ridden right over the last charge John had placed.

John and the others watched Scarns and his horse go up in the air, then come down separately.

As the sound of the final explosion rolled back in an echo from the canyon walls, the smoke began drifting away. Now, after several moments of rifle fire, dynamite charges, and cannon blasts, the battlefield was quiet.

A moment later it was obvious that the quiet was deceptive, because it was broken by the sobbing and groaning of wounded men. Those who weren't wounded were dead. Not one man of Scarns's attacking army remained upright.

"Whooeee!" Cap shouted, coming down from his gun emplacement. His face was blackened from powder. "Well, we did it to 'em, John, by gum!" he shouted gleefully. "Just like in the old days!"

Lonnie came limping over toward Slocum. "We did it," he said, a broad smile on his face. "We really did it."

"Oh, John, I was so scared!" Mindy shouted, rushing up to throw herself into his arms. "But I felt the excitement, too! It was wonderful and awful, at the same time!"

John embraced Mindy, then looked over at Lonnie.

When Mindy realized what she was doing, she kissed John, then moved over to throw her arms around Lonnie. "You were wonderful, Lonnie," she said.

"So were you." Lonnie smiled happily.

"Hell, we were all wonderful!" Cap added, and the four of them laughed.

Jimmy and Brad came riding in then, and they dismounted and walked over to join the four celebrants.

"How'd you do?" Cap asked.

"Nobody got away," Brad said.

"Good, good," Cap said. "You boys did great!"

"We lost Burt," Jimmy said.

"Lost 'im?"

"Dead," Jimmy said. "He went down with the first volley."

"I'm sorry to hear that," Cap said. "Burt was a good man."

"He died doin' what he wanted to do, Cap," Brad

Estes explained. "He's a good man and we hate to lose him, but he didn't die for nothin'. Scarns is dead. You won't be havin' no more trouble from the likes of him."

"No, I guess not," Cap said.

Slocum frowned.

"What is it?" Mindy asked, surprised by his change of expression. "What's the matter?"

"Nothing," Slocum said. "I was just thinking. When word of this gets out, nobody will ever think of doing this again."

"So?" asked a puzzled Cap.

"So, maybe we ought to make sure that word gets out. Get a wagon and we'll load these fellows in it, both the quick and the dead, and take 'em into town, bury them in Boot Hill in a common grave, and put a big sign on it, like a tombstone."

"Damned good idea!" cackled Cap.

"What would the sign say?" Lonnie wanted to know.

"Here lie the last rustlers ever to get buried in Sixgun Cemetery."

"Let's drink on it," Cap offered.

Arm-in-arm, the victorious warriors marched to the house.

GREAT WESTERN YARNS FROM ONE OF THE
BEST-SELLING WRITERS IN THE FIELD TODAY

JAKE LOGAN

____ 0-867-21003	**BLOODY TRAIL TO TEXAS**	$1.95
____ 0-867-21041	**THE COMANCHE'S WOMAN**	$1.95
____ 0-872-16979	**OUTLAW BLOOD**	$1.95
____ 0-425-06191-4	**THE CANYON BUNCH**	$2.25
____ 0-425-06255-4	**SLOCUM'S JUSTICE**	$2.25
____ 0-425-05958-8	**SLOCUM'S RAID**	$1.95
____ 0-872-16823	**SLOCUM'S CODE**	$1.95
____ 0-867-21071	**SLOCUM'S DEBT**	$1.95
____ 0-867-21090	**SLOCUM'S GOLD**	$1.95
____ 0-867-21023	**SLOCUM'S HELL**	$1.95
____ 0-867-21087	**SLOCUM'S REVENGE**	$1.95
____ 0-425-07665-2	**SLOCUM GETS EVEN**	$2.75
____ 0-425-06744-0	**SLOCUM AND THE** **LOST DUTCHMAN MINE**	$2.50
____ 0-425-06846-3	**GUNS OF THE SOUTH PASS**	$2.50

JAKE LOGAN

___ 07567-2	**SLOCUM'S PRIDE**	$2.50
___ 07382-3	**SLOCUM AND THE GUN-RUNNERS**	$2.50
___ 07494-3	**SLOCUM'S WINNING HAND**	$2.50
___ 08382-9	**SLOCUM IN DEADWOOD**	$2.50
___ 08279-2	**VIGILANTE JUSTICE**	$2.50
___ 08189-3	**JAILBREAK MOON**	$2.50
___ 08392-6	**SIX GUN BRIDE**	$2.50
___ 08076-5	**MESCALERO DAWN**	$2.50
___ 08539-6	**DENVER GOLD**	$2.50
___ 08644-X	**SLOCUM AND THE BOZEMAN TRAIL**	$2.50
___ 08742-5	**SLOCUM AND THE HORSE THIEVES**	$2.50
___ 08773-5	**SLOCUM AND THE NOOSE OF HELL**	$2.50
___ 08791-3	**CHEYENNE BLOODBATH**	$2.50
___ 09088-4	**THE BLACKMAIL EXPRESS**	$2.50
___ 09111-2	**SLOCUM AND THE SILVER RANCH FIGHT**	$2.50
___ 09299-2	**SLOCUM AND THE LONG WAGON TRAIN**	$2.50
___ 09212-7	**SLOCUM AND THE DEADLY FEUD**	$2.50
___ 09342-5	**RAWHIDE JUSTICE**	$2.50
___ 09395-6	**SLOCUM AND THE INDIAN GHOST**	$2.50
___ 09479-0	**SEVEN GRAVES TO LAREDO**	$2.50
___ 09567-3	**SLOCUM AND THE ARIZONA COWBOYS**	$2.50

Available at your local bookstore or return this form to:

BERKLEY
THE BERKLEY PUBLISHING GROUP, Dept. B
330 Murray Hill Parkway, East Rutherford, NJ 07073

Please send me the titles checked above. I enclose _____ Include $1.00 for postage and handling if one book is ordered; add 25¢ per book for two or more not to exceed $1.75. CA, IL, NJ, NY, PA, and TN residents please add sales tax. Prices subject to change without notice and may be higher in Canada. Do not send cash.

NAME_____

ADDRESS_____

CITY_____ STATE/ZIP_____

(Allow six weeks for delivery.)

162b

45